LOVE, LUCAS

LOVE, LUCAS

CHANTELE SEDGWICK

Sky Pony Press
New York

Sky Pony Press books may be purchased in bulk at special discounts for sales promotion, corporate gifts, fund-raising, or educational purposes. Special editions can also be created to specifications. For details, contact the Special Sales Department, Sky Pony Press, 307 West 36th Street, 11th Floor, New York, NY 10018 or info@skyhorsepublishing.com.

Sky Pony® is a registered trademark of Skyhorse Publishing, Inc.®, a Delaware corporation.
Visit our website at www.skyponypress.com.

10 9 8 7 6 5 4 3 2 1

Library of Congress Cataloging-in-Publication Data is available on file.

Cover design by Erin Seaward-Hiatte
Cover photo credit: Shutterstock

Print ISBN: 978-1-63220-417-2
Ebook ISBN: 978-1-63450-003-6

Printed in the United States of America

To Chakell,
who loved this book first.

Acknowledgments

This book is so special to me for so many reasons and there's no way it could have gotten out into the world without some amazing people by my side.

To my wonderful hardworking agent, Nicole Resciniti, who believed in Oakley's story and who continues to believe in me.

To my editor, Nicole Frail, whom I adore. Thank you for loving this story as much as I do and for helping me shape it into something beautiful. Thank you also to everyone behind the scenes at Sky Pony. I sincerely appreciate everything you have done for me.

To my fabulous critique partners and best friends, Katie Dodge and Ruth Josse. Thank you. For everything. I don't know where I would be without you two.

To Jessie Humphries for giving me surfing lessons through Facebook messages and for always making me laugh at your inappropriateness. Haha.

Thank you to the rest of my awesome and hilarious writing group: Peggy Eddleman, Erin Summerill, Kim Krey, Taffy Lovell, Jeigh Meredith, Shelly Brown, Donna Nolan, Julianne Donaldson, Jamie Thompson, and Christene

Houston for the writing retreats, sprints, get-togethers, and road trips.

To my beta readers, Megan Park and Michelle Argyle, for your fabulous critiques to make this book better.

To my parents, Robert and Cheri Wardleigh, for always believing in me and supporting me ever since I was a kid, even if my dreams and ideas seemed a little crazy.

To my brother, Braeden Wardleigh, for being my Lucas.

To my sisters, Chaleese Leishman and Chakell Wardleigh, for being my best friends and for reading every single draft of everything I write, even when it sucks.

A huge thank-you to Daniel Sedgwick for answering all of my random medical questions. And the rest of my family who have supported me on this journey, I'm truly grateful.

And finally, to the loves of my life. My husband, David, who told me to chase my dreams and has supported me so much since I started writing so many years ago. I love you.

To my four beautiful and crazy kidlets, Caden, Kinley, Brooklyn, and Beckam, who keep me on my toes and brighten every single day.

And last but not least, to my readers. Thank you for taking a chance on me and Oakley's story. I hope you love Lucas as much as I do.

LOVE,
LUCAS

CHAPTER 1

Everyone tells me funerals help with the grieving process, but I think those people are full of crap. If anything, they make you more depressed than you already are.

I stare at my brother's casket as we gather around the gravesite. A few inches of snow covers the ground around us and I shiver at the cold breeze biting at my skin. Dad blows his nose and I glance over and see Mom crying into the shoulder of his coat. I'm not sure how she even has tears left.

I know I'm supposed to feel something. Anything. Relief that Lucas is out of pain. Anger that he was taken so early from us. Sadness that I'll never hear his laugh or see his smiling face again.

Instead I feel only a hollow emptiness inside my chest. He took part of me with him. I can already feel the hole he left behind, waiting for something to fill it. But I know no one can ever take the place of my best friend.

Mom grabs my arm and gives it a squeeze. She holds out a tissue but I don't take it. I haven't cried since the night at the hospital. The night he left us. I know so much emotion is built up inside of me, looking for a chance to escape, but for some reason I can't, no, *won't* let it out. Something's wrong with me.

Dad wraps an arm around my waist. I don't move. My arms are like weights at my side. Lifeless. Like Lucas.

Mom says something to me and presses a long stemmed rose into my hand. I stare at it and say nothing. I've always hated flowers at funerals. They're supposed to make you feel happy. Not depressed.

People around me move one by one toward the casket and place their roses on top. As I watch them, my fist closes and I crush the delicate petals of my flower into my palm. The maimed rose slides from my fingers and drops to the ground.

I can't handle this. Everyone is so sad. Red faces, puffy eyes. The world seems to move in slow motion as Dad places his rose on the casket. Mom does the same. My breath catches as I notice everyone staring at me, waiting for me to do something. Anything.

Dad urges me forward to take my turn, but my feet refuse to move. He keeps his hand on my back and I take a deep breath before I look up at him. His eyes are sad as they fall on the pieces of the rose at my feet. He doesn't say anything about it, just grabs my hand and meets my gaze, but the look he gives me while his eyes fill with tears is more than I can handle. I have to get out of here. I step away from him, take one last look at the casket, and turn around.

"Oakley? Where are you going?" Dad asks.

I don't answer, just push past him and move through the crowd as my heart hammers in my chest.

Mom calls my name. Dad calls for me, too. I keep walking and don't look back.

CHAPTER 2

My parents are arguing again. Mom quit her job at the bank. It didn't go over very well with Dad, who has thrown himself into his job like a madman. I know they're both grieving in their own ways but they should talk to each other about it, not fight. Fighting gets you nowhere.

I listen to their raised voices for a moment and put on my headphones when Mom starts crying. I can't handle hearing her sob all night again, so I turn my iPod on and music blasts in my ears. Nothing like a bunch of guitars and screaming to drown out my parents and my own thoughts. If I can't hear them, they're not there.

I lie on my bed and stare at the glow-in-the-dark stars that light up the ceiling. Lucas bought them for me for my sixteenth birthday. He even made his own constellation out of them and called it Luca Major. Stupid, but funny. It makes me miss him even more.

The light flips on and I turn my head to see Mom standing in the doorway. I pause my music and sit up.

"Sorry," she says. "I knocked, but you didn't answer."

I shrug. "It's fine." My voice is hoarse. It was so hard for me to say those two words. I haven't spoken since the funeral three days ago, and no one's really spoken to me either.

She hesitates in the doorway but finally comes to sit on the edge of my bed. "Oakley," she starts. She takes a deep breath and reaches out to tuck my dark hair behind my ear. I pull away from her touch. After all the time and energy she's spent on my brother the past few years, it's foreign to me. "Your father and I have been talking. I've decided to go live with Aunt Jo for a while. Maybe just until summer. I need some time . . ." She swallows and blinks back the moisture in her eyes. "I need time away from here for a while."

"Okay . . ." I say. Great. She's abandoning me. First Lucas, now her. I breathe in and out. I still don't feel much. Just empty.

"I wanted to see if . . . well . . ." She smoothes my hair down, and though I consider protesting, I let her. "Honey, I want you to come with me."

My heart races. "You're not getting divorced, are you?" I pray she says no. I can't handle anything else going wrong. Not now. Not when I need at least some normalcy in my life.

She shakes her head. "No. Your father and I are fine. We just . . . grieve differently." The way she says it confirms that they're not *fine*. She takes a shaky breath. "Anyway, just think about coming with me, okay? You don't have to be in school since you graduated early, and you don't have a job or anything. I think it could be good for you to get away from everything."

4

I think about her offer. Even though I'll miss Dad, I'd love to get away. I could leave my depressing life behind for the spring and maybe heal a little before I have to decide what to do with my life. College and all that crap. I'll leave my house and put all the memories of Lucas and my old friends and their whispers behind my back. It would be nice to get away from it all. Away from the uncomfortable silence whenever I see anyone who knows me. I know they aren't sure what to say; I mean, what do you say to someone who just lost her brother? Even if they have something to say, I'm not sure I'd want to hear it anyway.

"Remember, Jo lives in California now, if that makes a difference. Huntington Beach. She has a really nice house with room to spare."

I crack a smile. It feels strange on my lips but it's a start. If I go with Mom, I could use my camera again. The thought of taking pictures comforts me. Just a little. I turn toward her and meet her eyes. "Okay," I whisper.

She puts her arms around me in an awkward hug. I'm not sure what to do with my own arms, so I lift one and softly pat her back. Physical contact has been nonexistent with her for a while now. She's not the touchy-feely type. We get along well enough, but for her to hug me . . . I'm sure it takes a lot.

"We're going to be okay," she says. It sounds like she's trying to reassure herself more than me. She pulls away, pats my leg, and stands. "We're leaving tomorrow morning, so you'd better start packing. I've already booked the flights."

I frown. That doesn't surprise me at all. "So . . . you

were going to drag me there whether I wanted to go or not?"

She shrugs. "I think it will be good for you. For us."

I want to say something else but don't have the energy as thoughts of Lucas pop into my head again. Instead, I swallow the lump in my throat, give her a quick nod, and she leaves me alone.

Spending the next few months with Aunt Jo might be a good thing. She's a marine biologist or veterinarian or something, so maybe she'll distract me with some of her work. And I've never been to a real beach before since our family doesn't really leave the state of Utah. The only beachy place I've been is Antelope Island. This tiny island in the middle of the Great Salt Lake that's covered with mosquitoes, flies, and brine shrimp. As for animals, I'm sure there are a few antelope here and there, but I've never seen any. Just a whole lot of buffalo. Antelope Island . . . covered in buffalo. Go figure.

A real beach. The thought sounds amazing. I've only seen pictures of Aunt Jo in the ocean. I'd love to have some photos of my own to hang on my wall. I climb off my bed and go look for a suitcase. Tomorrow can't come soon enough.

My ears pop as we land in California. Mom grabs her carry-on from the overhead compartment and passes me my guitar. I already have my backpack on my lap. We both keep our jumbled thoughts to ourselves. When the line starts to move, I stand, and we follow the crowd and exit the stuffy plane.

Aunt Jo is waiting for us at baggage claim. She runs to Mom and they hug forever, even though they saw each other at the funeral four days ago. Everyone around us is staring, so I move away from them and wait for our suitcases to come down the chute and onto the turnstile. I don't want to talk about Lucas, so I let them have a moment to themselves.

"How are you doing, Oakley? You hangin' in there?"

I flinch at Jo's hand on my shoulder. "I'm good." I grab my suitcase and she lets go. I don't miss the look she gives Mom.

They're worried about me. They can see through the fake smile I put on for everyone who asks how I'm doing. I don't know why I pretend everything's okay when clearly it's not. Lucas is gone. How can anything be okay when he's not here? He was the only person in my life I could count on.

"Oakley, honey, you ready?" Mom looks over at me with a sad but hopeful smile.

"Yes." I throw my backpack over my shoulder and my guitar over the other and follow them to the car, dragging my suitcase behind me.

The drive to Jo's house is quiet. I study her and my mom for a while. It's weird that they're even sisters. They look nothing alike. Mom's short dark hair is neat and straight, while Jo's is long with light wild curls. Mom is pale with soft skin, and Jo is tan and rough-looking from being outside all the time. I look like Mom. Dark hair and pale skin. Sort of like death.

They're so different. Their lives especially. Mom married Dad when she was only nineteen. They were high school sweethearts. Obviously it isn't working out too well. I wonder why Jo never married, but I don't ask. I'm not in the mood for conversation.

Jo's house is beautiful. It's right across the street from the beach. There are windows everywhere. Huge rectangular windows that face the ocean. I've always dreamed of living in a house like this. It seems so peaceful. Safe from whispers and gossip. Just what I need.

"You like it?" Jo asks.

I meet her eyes in the rearview mirror and smile. "It's perfect."

She puts the car in park and glances at Mom for a second before looking at me again. "I fixed one of the guest rooms up for you so you'll have some privacy while you're here. I remember what it was like being a teenager. And your mom told me you like your space. Hopefully you can call it your home away from home for a while." She gives me a wink before she gets out.

I open the door and step outside as well, breathing in the salty air. It's strange and different from what I'm used to back home, but right and wonderful at the same time. This is where I'm supposed to be right now and I'm so happy I came.

Palm trees peak around the edge of the house and I have the sudden desire to climb one. I breathe in the ocean air again and grin. For some reason I feel lighter than before. Like all my troubles will magically melt away the moment I step into that beautiful house. But as memories of the past few weeks slam into me again, I realize the depressing fact that fantasy never wins over reality. Even when it should.

We unload our bags and I follow Jo and Mom up the front steps. Jo opens the door and Mom steps back so I can go in first. My jaw drops as I look around.

The inside is gorgeous. Sunlight spills in through the windows, making it almost as bright as outside. The rooms are open. Not stuffy or crowded, but roomy. I'm surprised by Jo's color choice. The furniture is white, with yellow flowers and throw pillows to accent the living room. A perfect choice for a house like this.

I drop my bags near the door for a moment and take my time walking around the front room, admiring the little seashells accenting the tables. Of course they're not plastic. They're very real, and that makes me happy.

Mom's heels click on the white tile floor and echo through the house. She turns around and smiles. "Jo, I love it," she says. "It's amazing."

"Thanks. It was a bunch of work fixing it up, but I think it turned out nicely." Jo smiles and turns to me. "Your room is the last one on the left if you want to check it out."

I grab my bags as I make my way down the hall and open my bedroom door. My eyes widen as I see how big it is. A bed dominates most of the room, with a dresser and mirror across from it. The same sort of decorations are in here as well. Seashells on the glass nightstand near the bed and a few pictures of the ocean hung up on the walls. I throw my backpack on the ground and set my guitar on the bed. My fingers skim the pretty white bedspread. It's not quite my style, since my room back home is decorated with orange, pink, and lime green, but it works.

I glance around and notice a walk-in closet. Nice. Not that I have a ton of clothes, but still. My favorite part of the room is the French doors that lead outside to a small covered patio. I peek out the window and grin. There's a hammock and lounge chair and a huge swimming pool. It's nice and blue. Clean. I wonder if Jo has a pool man, since she obviously makes a ton of money to live in a place like this.

I walk around for a while and go through the fence to the front yard. It's surreal to be so close to the ocean. My feet start walking on their own and I cross the street and head toward the sand and waves. My first time ever at a beach, and I've heard Huntington is really nice.

My flip-flops are covered in sand so I slip them off. I smile at the feel of the sand between my toes. Again, I feel safe. Free. Ready for a new beginning.

The beach is different than I imagined. In all the pictures I've seen, there are always a ton of people lying on the sand, tanning. I look around. There aren't a lot of people out at all. At least not today. An older couple sits a few yards away under big umbrellas. The lady is reading a book and the man I assume is her husband is taking a nap. A few people are playing volleyball further down the beach and there are some surfers bobbing in the water.

It's like heaven. I walk until I feel the icy ocean water touch my feet. It sends a little shock through my body, but I don't care. It's awesome. After a few minutes of watching the tiny waves roll up around my ankles while my feet sink into the mud, I walk back up the beach and sit down in the sand. It's warm, but a cool breeze caresses my skin. Fascinated, I watch the waves crash into the beach and the surfers riding them so effortlessly.

I sink my toes deeper into the sand and smile. I think I'm going to like it here.

CHAPTER 3

Mom wakes me from a deep sleep. I know it's her by the way she rubs little circles on my back. My mind is fuzzy, but I manage a groan and roll over in an attempt to get away from her. She lets out a soft sigh. "Oakley, wake up. I need to talk to you," she says.

"Leave me alone," I whisper.

It's been two days since we got here. Two days, and all I've done is lie in my room staring at the wall. The reality of losing Lucas has settled around me like a dark, suffocating cloud and won't let me go. I know I'm suffering from some kind of depression but the thought of doing something about it makes me tired. I can't handle a shrink right now.

Mom keeps rubbing my back but I ignore her. Last night was the first time I slept all night. I haven't slept well since Lucas was admitted to the hospital. It feels like forever ago. I close my eyes again, trying to remember the dream I was having. It was a good dream. I remember feeling happy.

"Please, Oakley. Just look at me for a second."

I let out an annoyed breath and roll to face her. Her dark eyes are worried, like she's afraid if she looks away, I'll disappear or something. "I told you last night, I'm fine. I'm just catching up on some sleep."

"No, it's not about that. I have something for you."

"What?"

She bites her lip. "Honey," she says. Her voice shakes and I sit up, wondering why she sounds so nervous. "I . . . um . . ." There's a small notebook in her hand and she hands it to me. "Lucas asked me to give this to you. Before he died." Her voice shakes on the last word.

I freeze. "What is it?"

She shrugs. "It's for you. He wanted you to read it."

I take it. It's one of those black-and-white composition notebooks that I used in a few classes at school. My name is written on the front in his handwriting. I run my fingertips over it, not sure if I want to open it and read the contents. I'm still feeling so many emotions and if this is his journal about the last days of his life or something . . . I don't think I'll be able to handle it.

"Have you—"

"No." She shakes her head. "I haven't looked at it."

"Oh." I believe her, but for some reason it makes me more nervous. Why would he leave something like this just for me? Did he have some deep, dark secrets he was keeping and wanted to tell me them after he died? And why did Mom give it to me now? "How long have you had this?"

"I've had it since the funeral. Or . . . a few days before, I guess. He told me to give it to you after you had some time to . . ." She swallows and looks away. "Anyway. I'll leave you alone." Mom steps away from me, her eyes on the notebook. She looks sad. Her fingers drum on the doorframe a second before she grabs the doorknob. "Jo and I are going to run to the store. We won't be gone long."

"Okay," I say.

"You sure you'll be okay without me?" Her voice sounds far away as I stare at the notebook I'm clutching.

I tear my gaze away from my name and look at her. "I'll be fine, Mom." I smile to make her believe me and she nods and closes the door. I look back at the notebook. I'm intrigued and scared at the same time.

My hands are shaking. I'm still not sure I can handle what's written inside. I have to know, though, so I take a deep breath and flip it open. The letter on the first page is in his handwriting as well. I always made fun of him for writing in all capital letters. I think it's a guy thing because Dad does it too.

DEAR OAKLEY,
    THAT SOUNDS SO FORMAL, DOESN'T IT?

I laugh. Lucas wasn't formal at all.

TODAY WE FOUND OUT MY CANCER IS TERMINAL. YOU TOOK IT WAY HARDER THAN ME. I KNEW IT WAS COMING, BUT I THINK YOU STILL HAD HOPE THAT I'D BEAT THIS. I'M SORRY YOU WERE SO UPSET. YOU KNOW I WOULD CHANGE THINGS IF I COULD. WHICH IS IMPOSSIBLE, BUT YOU KNOW I'D TRY.

ANYWAY, I'VE DECIDED TO DO SOMETHING FOR YOU. IF YOU'RE READING THIS, I'M ALREADY GONE. I KNEW YOU'D HAVE A HARD TIME WITH ME DYING. PROBABLY MORE THAN ANYONE. DON'T LIE AND SAY YOU'RE FINE. I KNOW YOU BETTER THAN THAT.

THE REASON I'M WRITING THIS NOTEBOOK IS SO YOU CAN HAVE A PIECE OF ME WITH YOU ALL THE TIME. IT'S LAME, BUT IT'S SOMETHING, RIGHT? YOU CAN READ IT ALL RIGHT NOW, OR YOU CAN READ ONE ENTRY EVERY DAY. IT'S SORT OF LIKE A JOURNAL, BUT MOSTLY MY STUPID RANDOM THOUGHTS. I WANT YOU TO REMEMBER THE GOOD THINGS. THE IMPORTANT THINGS. ME. HOPEFULLY SOME OF MY THOUGHTS WILL MAKE SENSE. ACTUALLY, OF COURSE THEY WILL. YOU KNOW HOW AWESOME I AM.

ANYWAY I LOVE YOU, OAKLEY. IF THERE IS ONE THING I WANT YOU TO KNOW, THAT'S IT. YOU'RE MY BEST FRIEND AND I'LL MISS YOU MORE THAN WORDS CAN SAY.

STAY STRONG.

LOVE, LUCAS

My eyes burn but I manage to hold back my emotions. Lucas always knows what to say. Always. Even when he isn't here anymore.

I look around my temporary room with a sense of longing. I don't have anyone to talk to. No one to call. It's the first time I realize I'm totally alone. My parents don't seem to want to talk to me about anything, my friends abandoned me back home—or I guess I abandoned them—and Lucas is gone. I have no one to turn to.

No one. And it hurts so much it takes my breath away. I close my eyes and try to get hold of myself. It's hard, but I manage.

My fingers tremble as I close the notebook. I'll read one entry every day. I don't want to waste the whole thing in one sitting because I want to savor each word and phrase. I put it under my pillow for later.

My stomach growls but I ignore it and go sit on my porch swing outside. I take a deep breath. I can't get over how good the salty air smells. It calms me.

It's early Thursday morning but as I walk around to the front yard there are a lot of people already on the boardwalk. I sit on the porch and watch them riding bikes, Rollerblading, and running. I didn't know people still went Rollerblading. It seems so long ago since I tried. I still remember Rollerblading with Lucas at the neighbor's house when we were little. They had a big driveway and we would pretend we were professional ice-skaters. I'm sure we looked ridiculous but we didn't care.

I look past the people on the boardwalk and I'm surprised I can see a bunch of surfers in the water, even from where I sit.

Intrigued, and admittedly tired of lying around, I decide to go take some pictures and grab my camera bag and a beach blanket before heading across the street.

The sand is warm between my toes as I stroll toward the waves. I stop a few yards from the water and spread my blanket out, stretch my legs in front of me, and sit back and watch the show.

As soon as I get comfortable, a girl to the left of me laughs and I look over to see a group of teenagers in wet suits headed into the water with surfboards in hand. The girl has a ring through her nose and long blonde hair hanging down her back. She lets out a laugh and nudges the guy next to her with her shoulder before pulling her hair into a ponytail. I can't help but stare. They look so carefree. So . . . normal.

A guy in the group, tan with dark hair, catches my eye and grins at me before turning to his friends again. I feel my cheeks heat and shake my head. I'm such a dork.

In seconds, the group is paddling out into the ocean. I watch them spread out and suck in a breath as the girl with the nose ring gets up on a wave like it's nothing. I'm mesmerized. She knows exactly what she's doing in the water. Her whole body is relaxed, and I swear she skims the inside of the wave with her fingers. I can't help myself; I pull my camera out and snap a few photos of her before she disappears into the water.

My skin's burning from the sun but I don't care. I could use some color. If only I had gotten Dad's skin, then I'd be a true tan California girl. Instead I'm a pasty white ghost from Utah.

I take a few more pictures before getting distracted by an outcrop of rocks a little way down the beach. There are people wandering around them, a few kneeling and pointing into the water. Curious, I head their way, leaving my blanket on the sand, but taking my camera bag with me.

The rocks are bigger than I thought they would be and they're brown and slick. My bare feet make it hard to climb, but I sling my bag over my shoulder and figure it out. Once I pull my body up onto the rock, I smile. There are tide pools all around me, full of different sea creatures left by the tide.

I peek into the nearest tide pool and see a few starfish stuck to the nearest rock—a yellow one and a red one missing a limb. They're strange creatures, starfish. When I was a kid, Jo came to visit and took us to an aquarium. I remember she flipped one over and made me touch its little feet. It had grossed me out and I'm pretty sure I ran away screaming. For some reason, the memory makes me want to pick one up.

I glance in the water again and notice a third starfish. This one's orange and flipped upside down in the sand at the bottom of the tide pool. I set my camera bag down, slide onto my belly, and reach into the cool water to rescue it. As I pull it out, I scoot back and study my new friend.

It's just like I remember: hard and bumpy on one side and slimy and suctiony on the other. The little feet wiggle around as I poke and prod—nicely, of course. After I've finished examining, I scoot back to the edge of the pool and put the little guy back in the water. I smile as it floats to the bottom like a snowflake. I grab my camera bag and pull out my camera to take a few pictures. I'm leaning forward, snapping a few of the two starfish still attached to the wall, when someone speaks.

"Something must be pretty interesting in there."

I stand up so fast I lose my balance and almost drop my camera. My foot slips off the edge and splashes into the water. I would have fallen all the way in, but a strong hand grabs my arm and pulls me out.

I brush my hair out of my face and look up into a pair of chocolate eyes. "Sorry about that. Didn't mean to scare you."

I can't help but stare. He's cute—light brown hair, probably six feet tall I'd guess, since I have to look up at him. He's alone, which is weird. I've noticed that usually people walk around the beach as couples or in groups. But I'm alone, so I guess I'm weird too.

"Are you okay?" he asks. A mix of humor and concern cross his features as his dark eyes take me in.

"I'm . . . uh . . . I'm fine." I cringe at my choice of words. Yay for me. I just sounded like an idiot. And why do I always say everything is fine? I need to think of some other phrase to use. "Thanks."

He's still holding onto my wrist. I yank my arm away—harder than I mean to—since I have no idea who he is. He gives me a strange look and my cheeks warm. I have the sudden urge to throw myself into the ocean and sink to the bottom. I've never been very good around guys. *Awkward* would be the right word for it. I didn't date at all back home since I spent every spare moment at the hospital with Lucas. I've never kissed anyone either. How could I think of myself when Lucas was so sick for so long? It didn't make sense to date and be happy when Lucas was fighting for his life.

He's watching me. I hope he's not waiting for me to say something, because I really have no idea *what* to say.

"You like photography?" He gestures to the camera dangling in my hand.

I let out the breath I'm holding and nod, taking in his tanned skin. His light shirt clings to his body and I can see muscles peeking out from beneath his sleeves. A surfer maybe? I wonder if he's a local.

He laughs. "That was a stupid question, wasn't it? Of course you like photography. You're out here taking pictures with a camera that's probably worth more than my car."

I smile and fiddle with the lens cover. The camera's not that expensive, but it wasn't cheap either. I worked all summer last year at a local restaurant to save up for it.

He's still watching me. And I still have no idea what to say to him, which is stupid. He seems nice. It's times like these I wish I were more like Lucas. I swear every time we went to the grocery store, he made a best friend in the checkout line.

"Are you on vacation? I haven't seen you around here before."

So he *is* a local. Not sure if that's a good thing or not. After clearing my throat, I finally get the courage to speak. "I'm staying with my aunt for a few months. Jocelyn Reynolds?" I point in the direction of her house.

His face seems to light up. "Jo's your aunt? She's awesome!"

"You know her?"

He shrugs. "Everyone around here knows her. I live next door to her, though, so I know her a little better than most. She's great. She takes me and my friends on her boat a lot. We help her out at work sometimes. I'm trying to get an internship with her for the summer." He looks out into the water. "She took us out to see some sharks last week. It was pretty sweet."

I have no clue what he's talking about, since I don't know exactly what Jo does for her job, but I nod anyway. "Cool. I'm going to have to ask her about taking me out on her boat sometime. I don't think I'd like seeing sharks though. They freak me out."

"They aren't that bad. They're just as scared of us as we are of them."

"I doubt that," I say, smiling. "Everyone always says that about wasps and hornets, yet they still find a reason to sting people." I feel my uneasiness slipping away, which makes me feel a little better.

He laughs, louder this time. He has a nice laugh. "You're funny. I'm Carson, by the way." He extends his hand and I take it. It's callused and his handshake is strong compared to my wimpy grip.

"Oakley," I say. "Oakley Nelson."

He raises an eyebrow and lets his hand fall to his side. "That's an interesting name. I can honestly say I've never met an Oakley before."

I'm not sure if he means that in a good way or bad.

"I like it," he says, smiling. I notice a dimple in his left cheek. He's still staring and I look away, feeling a smile creep in. It feels good to smile.

"Carson! Where've you been, man? The waves are killer out there. Did you see that sick set?"

The surfer I saw earlier is coming out of the water. He shakes his dark hair, sending droplets flying in every direction. He notices me and I swear he stands up straighter. He flexes his toned chest and I try really hard not to stare. I fail, like any other girl would. Embarrassed, I lean down and grab my camera case. I should put my camera away before I drop it or something. And to avoid staring.

"Dillon, this is Oakley. Oakley, Dillon," Carson says.

I look up. "Hi," I manage. He's cute, with strong features, complete with a cleft in his chin. The kind of guy all the girls would be after in my high school.

He brushes his wet hair out of his eyes. "I saw you this morning at Jo's place. You livin' there?"

"Yeah. For a little bit," I say.

"Cool." He glances at Carson but his body stays turned toward me. "So, what's up with you, Carson? Your foot still bothering ya?"

Carson chuckles. "I'm fine. Just thought I'd skip out for today." He shifts his weight and winces.

I peer down and notice he's wearing flip-flops, but his left foot is wrapped in a bandage. Like it's sprained or something.

"Dude. You're lame." Dillon looks me over again and runs a hand through his hair. "If you want to get to know some of our crowd, we're having a bonfire on the beach tonight. Hot dogs, s'mores, a couple kegs. Wanna come?"

"You should. It'll be fun," Carson says.

I open my mouth but nothing comes out. I don't even know these people and they're already inviting me to a party? Where the heck am I?

I hear Carson shift on the rock next to me. "We don't bite," he says. "And if you're going to be here for a few months, you should get to know some of us locals. There'll be a bunch of girls there too. Not just us. If that makes you feel any better."

They both stare at me, waiting for my answer, and I start to panic. "Um . . . probably not tonight. I have . . . uh . . . stuff to do. Thanks, though." I put my camera bag over my shoulder and climb back down to the sand.

"It was awesome to meet you," Dillon says. He winks at me and starts back toward the water.

Really? Who winks?

"It's at seven if you change your mind," Carson yells at my back.

I don't respond or look at them again; I'm too busy trying to figure out what the heck is wrong with me.

CHAPTER 4

We sit at the kitchen table in silence. Mom watches me as I push my mashed potatoes around my plate. I know that look. It's her worried-but-too-afraid-to-say-anything look. "So, he asked you to go to a party and you said no?"

I sigh. I've already told her the story. Three times. "Yes, Mom. I said no."

"Why?"

"Why do you care?" I snap. Why *does* she care?

Her eyes grow wide but she doesn't yell. Instead, she shrugs. "I think it's nice. It would be good for you to meet some new friends."

"I'm fine, Mom. I have my own friends at home. I don't need new ones." We both know it's a lie. I haven't talked to my friends back home in months. I feel a pang in my chest as I think of my best friends Emmy and Kelsie. I should have at least said goodbye.

Jo comes in the room then glances at both of us. "What's going on?"

"Some guy asked Oakley on a date and she said no."

"Mom," I groan. "It wasn't a date!"

"Who?" Jo asks, smiling. "You haven't even been here a week and guys are already hitting on you?"

I try not to smile but fail. "No. He wasn't hitting on me. He was just being nice."

I'm quiet as I mix my corn and potatoes together. They're better that way, Lucas always said. Not that I'll eat them, since I haven't had an appetite in I don't know how long, but I can't break the habit.

My fork clinks against my plate, the only sound in the room. Mom and Jo's silence is getting on my nerves but I don't say anything. I don't want to talk about Carson anymore and I know that's what they're after.

"So, who was it?" Jo asks.

"Seriously? It's not a big deal."

"Oh, come on. Just give me a name." She glances at Mom and grins. "There aren't that many locals around here. Maybe I know him."

I let out a huge exaggerated sigh. "Fine. I met a guy by the tide pools this morning. His name was Carson. Happy now?"

"Carson Nye?"

I shrug. "I never asked him his last name, but he said he knows you."

"It has to be him." She smiles. "He's a good kid. Lives next door." She studies me for a moment and I shrink under her gaze. "You should go."

"I'm not going."

"Why?"

"Because it would be weird. I don't even know him. I talked to him for like, two seconds."

Jo snorts. "Well, obviously he wants to get to know you, or he wouldn't have asked you to go."

I roll my eyes. "Whatever." I take a bite of broccoli. I don't like broccoli. How did it even get on my plate? I chew really fast and eat a piece of chicken to cover up the horrible taste in my mouth.

Mom frowns. "Honey, you should go. Go have fun. I'm worried about you. Ever since Lucas . . ." Her voice squeaks as she says his name. She clears her throat and takes a shaky breath. "Ever since we lost Lucas, you've built a wall around yourself. Maybe if you make some friends, you could be yourself again."

My hand stops halfway to my mouth and I slowly set my fork down. "Mom, I'm fine."

"You're not. You're not yourself, Oakley. Lying in bed all day? Doing nothing? It's not like you at all."

I push my chair back and stand up, furious at where the conversation is headed. "Who do you want me to be, Mom? The same as I was before? I can't just forget about everything and get over it like you can."

Her mouth drops open and I see the hurt in her eyes. "I haven't gotten over it," she whispers. "I lost my son, Oakley. And I don't want to lose my daughter too."

"Where do you think I'm going? I'm not suicidal, Mom. I told you. I'm fine. Just leave it alone."

"I didn't say you were suicidal." She sighs. "I'm just trying to help you. I want you to have friends. I want you to have a normal life again." She reaches out to touch me but I pull away. I don't understand where all of this is coming from. She's not supposed to care about me. She hasn't for months. And even if she did, she's had a funny way of showing it. "This is why we came here. To start over."

I frown. "I don't want to start over and I don't need your help. I don't need anybody." I turn away from her and go to my room, slamming the door behind me.

Why does she have to do that? Make me feel guilty for no reason. I'm fine. I told her so. I don't need friends. The only thing they would do is feel sorry for me anyway. I don't need anyone's pity. And if she's so worried about me, why hasn't she told me before? I needed her weeks ago. I needed her and she wasn't there.

Lucas's notebook is sitting on my bed. I walk over to it and pick it up, turning to page two. I told myself I'd only read one each day, but right now I'm throwing my plan out the window. I need my brother.

DEAR OAKLEY,

HA. IT'S KIND OF FUNNY WRITING "DEAR." YOU'RE MY SISTER, AND I'M NOT SENDING A RÉSUMÉ OR LETTER TO ANYONE SUPER IMPORTANT. NOT THAT YOU AREN'T IMPORTANT . . . OH, NEVER MIND. ANYWAY, TODAY IS THE DAY I START THIS STUPID NOTEBOOK FULL OF INSIGHTS INTO YOUR AWESOME BROTHER'S LIFE. I KNOW YOU'RE DYING TO FIND OUT WHAT GOES ON IN MY HEAD.

SO, TODAY, A NEW NURSE WAS ASSIGNED TO MY ROOM. SHE'S HOT AND I REALLY WANT TO ASK HER OUT. I'M PRETTY SURE SHE'S LIKE EIGHT YEARS OLDER THAN ME, WHICH COULD PROVE TO BE A CHALLENGE . . . BUT I'M NINETEEN, SO

SHE WOULDN'T GO TO JAIL IF WE DID END UP HOOKING UP. I WONDER IF SHE'LL GO OUT WITH ME. WE COULD HAVE A ROMANTIC DATE IN THE HOSPITAL CAFETERIA.

AND THAT, DEAR SISTER, IS A GLIMPSE INTO YOUR BROTHER'S MIND. PRETTY AWESOME, RIGHT? YOU LOVE IT.

OH, AND I'VE MADE A MENTAL NOTE TO LEAVE ONE THOUGHT FOR THE DAY IN EVERY LETTER. I GUESS I SHOULDN'T SAY EVERY LETTER, SINCE I'M SURE I'LL FORGET SOME. WITH THAT NOTE, TODAY'S THOUGHT IS BROUGHT TO YOU BY THE LETTER . . . JUST KIDDING. BUT FOR REAL. I KNOW YOU'RE GRIEVING. I KNOW IT'S HARD. BUT PLEASE DON'T GIVE UP ON LIFE. DON'T SHUT DOWN LIKE YOU ALWAYS DO WHEN SOMETHING GOES WRONG. GET OUT AND DO SOMETHING. GO FOR A WALK. PLAY YOUR GUITAR. DANCE AND SING—WELL, MAYBE NOT SING SINCE WE BOTH KNOW YOU SUCK, BUT YOU GET WHAT I'M TRYING TO SAY. DON'T SHUT DOWN. LIVE YOUR LIFE KNOWING YOU CAN GET OUT AND DO THINGS YOU WANT TO DO. I WISH I COULD.

LOVE, LUCAS

He knows me too well. *Get out and do something.* I can just hear him saying that. I close the notebook and slip it under my pillow again. *Don't shut down.* I'm not shutting down, am I? No, of course I'm not. I'll prove him wrong. I slide off my bed and go outside.

It's a beautiful night. Stars light the sky even though the sun hasn't set all the way yet. It's so peaceful here. There's music coming from the front yard, so I walk around and sit on one of the wicker chairs on the porch. I pull my legs up against my chest, wrap my arms around them, and lean my head back against the seat. The glow from the bonfire on the beach flickers through the dark and I'm surprised how many people are at Carson's party. I hear their muffled voices but can't pick out any intelligible words. Probably because I'm across the street. Duh.

A sense of longing comes over me. I wish I belonged somewhere. Anywhere.

A movement to my left makes me jump and I'm surprised when I realize who it is. Carson.

"Hey, Oakley." He walks around the porch and stops at the bottom of the stairs. "I was running late to the party and saw you sitting here by yourself. You still want to go? We can walk down together if you want."

I give him a small smile. "I'm not sure if I'm up to it tonight. Maybe next time. Thank you, though."

"You sure? If I'm being honest, you look like you need a friend tonight."

His smile is contagious and genuine. It makes me feel like he actually cares about me, even though he has no idea who I am.

But do I really look that depressed? "Really?"

"A little." He walks up the porch steps and leans against the wooden post holding up the awning. "Come on. It'll be fun. There will be food. And people. Nothing better than that." He studies me and I try not to stare back. "You don't have to if you don't want to."

I hesitate. "I'm not sure . . ." After blowing up at Mom, I don't really feel like doing anything. "I don't really know anyone."

He grins. "You know me."

I chuckle. "Kind of."

"Okay. You've got me there, but I promise I'm a nice guy." He walks, or rather limps, over to me and reaches out a hand. "Come with me. Nothing like a party on the beach on a night like this."

I stare at his hand. *Get out and do something.* Lucas's words invade my thoughts and I glance at the sky. I wonder if he's watching me from heaven like I'm on some reality show. Even though I miss him, I'm experiencing a really strong urge to flip him off. Which for some reason kind of puts me in a better mood. "You know, it *is* a nice night, isn't it?" I smile and grab Carson's hand and he pulls me out of the chair.

"Attagirl." He starts down the stairs but stops at the bottom. "Do you need to tell anyone where you're going?" He motions toward the house.

"Probably. Just a sec." I open the front door and poke my head inside. "Mom, I'm going out. I'll be back later."

I don't wait for her reply, just shut the door and head back outside. She wants me to make friends? Fine. I'll make friends.

Carson's waiting for me, and for the first time I notice his outfit: a red T-shirt and khaki shorts. He looks good in red. He's wearing flip-flops again, with his foot bandaged as it was before.

"You ready?" he asks.

I look down at my jeans and hoodie. I should probably change into something a bit nicer but I'm lazy. "Yep!" I give him a smile. He's so nice even though I totally don't deserve his niceness. Maybe, just maybe, I'll stop being ornery and enjoy myself tonight. Maybe.

"Great."

We cross the street and head down to the beach. I'm walking with my arms folded but drop them to my sides. I'm nervous but I don't want him to know that. "Thanks for walking me."

"No problem."

"So, what happened to your foot?"

He looks down at it and then over to me. "I got bit by a piece of coral. No big deal."

I smile. "You were surfing?"

He nods. "First time I've ever let the coral get the best of me. Ten stitches. It was pretty messed up, but I'll be back on the waves in a week or so."

"Ouch." I fold my arms. "You'd still surf with an injury like that?"

"This is nothing. A few of my buddies have gotten cut up pretty bad."

"Oh. It sounds painful."

He shrugs. "It's fine. I've had worse injuries than this."

"Really?"

"Broke my arm a few years ago. That hurt pretty bad."

"How did you break your arm?"

He shrugs. "Skateboarding."

"I can see that happening. Skateboarding is hard." I chuckle. "The only time I ever tried it, I ended up on my butt."

"Ha. I've done that plenty of times."

"How long have you been boarding?"

He grins. "Which kind?"

I shrug. "Both."

"Surfing since I was a kid, skateboarding since high school. I don't do that very often anymore though. Too many broken bones. Arm, wrist, dislocated shoulder. Good times."

"Seriously? I've never even broken one bone."

"Really?"

"Really. I've gotten stitches, though. My brother dared me to ride down a dirt hill on my bike and I fell off. The spiky part of the bike that holds the chain sliced my leg open. The crank, I think? I don't know bikes very well. Anyway, it was pretty bad. My brother felt awful. I actually did it the day before I started seventh grade. Great way to make an impression, right? A girl on crutches with a huge bandage on her leg." I point to the scar on my calf and he raises his eyebrows.

"That's quite the battle wound. It looks like an L."

I smile. Lucas always said my scar was shaped like an L because it was *his* fault and the universe wanted to remind him it was his fault forever. "I'm sure broken bones hurt worse."

He shrugs. "It's a toss-up, I think. My foot hurts pretty bad."

"It doesn't seem to bother you much."

"I like to act tougher than I really am."

I chuckle and he grins.

We reach the crowd of people around the bonfire and Carson reaches for my hand. I don't want to lose him, so I take it . . . and try not to overanalyze the gesture. He pulls me through the crowd and lets go when we reach a small group of people sitting around the fire.

"Hey, guys. This is Oakley." He stands to the side and shoves his hands in his pockets.

I recognize Dillon, who jumps to his feet and does a weird little bow in front of me. "Nice to see *you* again. I knew you'd change your mind and come." He grabs my hand and gives it a squeeze before sitting down again.

I give him a small smile.

I notice a few girls sitting next to him. They stare at me.

"Everyone, this is Oakley," Carson says.

The girls say hi but look more bored than anything. I recognize the girl from earlier. The one with the nose ring. She smiles at me and nods, then goes back to her conversation like I'm not even there. I look away. I've never had many girlfriends. I'm not sure why.

"You want a drink or anything?" Dillon asks. "There're a few beers left in the cooler." He reaches in and pulls one out to hand it to me.

I shake my head. "No thanks. I don't drink." I've never really thought about drinking. Especially since I was at the hospital with Lucas most of my high school days. I have to admit it's a little tempting now, though. I've always been the good girl. The one who never does anything wrong. I cross my arms. No. Not tonight. I don't want to make a fool of myself in front of all these people. And if Lucas really *is* watching me, he'd tell me not to be stupid.

His mouth falls open. "What? You don't drink?" He laughs and shakes his head. "She's as bad as you are, Carson."

I look over to find Carson smiling at me. I shrug and smile back. "I just like having complete control over my body at all times," Carson says.

By the way he looks at Dillon, I'm sure there's some kind of story that goes along with it, but I don't ask. I don't know these people, and I don't want to pry into their personal lives. That would just give them a reason to try to pry into mine.

Dillon snorts and opens a beer for himself instead. "You're getting boring in your old age."

"I'm the same age as you."

Dillon laughs. "You don't act like you're nineteen at all. You act like you're thirty. Lame."

We stand in awkward silence until Carson clears his throat. "Want a s'more? I roast a mean marshmallow."

"Sure."

He leads me over to a smaller fire and we sit down on an old log. He pulls a few marshmallows out of a bag and pushes them onto a long stick. "So, where're you from anyway? I'm guessing not anywhere close."

"I hail from Utah."

He laughs. "Never been there. Anything interesting I should know about?"

I slip off my flip-flops and bury my feet in the cool sand. "Not really. It's quiet for the most part. I think there are one or two families with younger kids in the neighborhood, but most of the people have lived there for years and are staying there forever. We have a lot of high schoolers and a lot of college students. Lots of colleges within driving distance, so a lot of the college students just live at home while they go to school."

He chuckles. "Kind of like here. Minus the school part."

I raise an eyebrow. I'm not sure what he means.

"We have a lot of college-aged people that live here and all they do is surf. Some of them go to school, but most locals just work here and surf every day. It's all they live for. The waves."

"Oh. Makes sense."

"Not that there's anything wrong with that, since I love surfing. I'd just like to get an education, you know? Do something with my life."

"What do you want to do?"

He smiles and I realize how amazing he looks in the firelight. His light hair looks darker and he swipes it out of his eyes. "I want to do what Jo does. Be a marine veterinarian. Rescue animals. I'd love to do that. There's nothing better than working with animals. And being out on the ocean would be a bonus."

"That does sound nice." I'll have to ask Jo more about her job. I thought she just worked in a lab or something, but it was starting to sound more interesting.

"So . . . do you have any plans for the future?" He grins and shakes his head. "I swear I don't ask boring questions all the time. At least I didn't ask you about the weather."

I laugh. "I have no idea what I want to do. I love photography but I haven't really thought about going into it. Like you, I like animals but I'm not sure if I could handle putting any to sleep. To be honest, I don't know if I want to go to college anytime soon. I'm kind of sick of school."

"Amen. So glad to be done with high school."

"Are you in college?"

He smiles, the dimple in his chin more pronounced. "Not yet. I could have gone this last year after I graduated, but I had a lot going on. I'm filling out applications for fall semester though."

"Ah. I see." I should probably fill some out too but college has been the last thing on my mind. I all but dropped out of high school a few months ago. Quit the swim team, student government. Everything. Mom finally put me on an accelerated program to get it over with and I ended up graduating in December. A whole semester before I was supposed to. Which turned out for the best. I refused to leave Lucas's side all through January, until we lost him on February 1. The worst day of my life.

"So, you weren't a fan of high school?" Carson's voice brings me back to the present.

"Not at all."

He hands me a box of graham crackers and a bar of chocolate. "I'm sure it wasn't that bad."

"It was. So much so, I graduated a few months ago. So glad I'm out of there." Everyone was weird around me. Even people who didn't know me very well were weird around me. Like I would break with the slightest touch. That's why I avoided everyone; I didn't want their pity.

He gives me a curious look but doesn't press for details. "So, you're seventeen then? Or eighteen?"

"Seventeen, I'll be eighteen in a few months."

"Nice." He turns his marshmallows around on his roasting stick. "It's cold in Utah right now, right?"

"Yep. February is still freezing cold. I love the snow at the beginning of winter, for a couple of weeks maybe, but I end up hating it after a while. The old black and crusty snow that doesn't melt for months gets kind of old. The first snow though, is like magic. I love going outside and listening to the quiet. Everything is so . . . still."

He nods. "I haven't seen snow forever. Not since I was a kid."

"Maybe I'll have my dad mail me some and you can look at it before it melts." I grin and he smiles back.

"Here. These marshmallows are about done." He moves the stick in front of me.

"Hold on a sec." I break a graham cracker in half and put some chocolate on the bottom cracker.

"Ready?"

I nod and squish the marshmallow between my two crackers. I hold it for a second to make sure the chocolate melts a little. It's no good when the chocolate is hard.

After waiting a moment or two, I take a bite. It's delicious. Melted chocolate drips onto my wrist and I lick it off, trying to ignore the smile Carson's giving me.

"You cooked this marshmallow to perfection. I'm impressed."

He beams. "I told you I could roast a mean marshmallow."

"Indeed you did." I don't like marshmallows plain, but I love toasted ones, especially on s'mores. They remind me of camping with my family. With Lucas. I stare at the fire, crackling and spitting in front of me, remembering how many times Lucas and I stayed up late, sitting around the campfire telling ghost stories and scaring the crap out of each other. We always had so much fun until we had to go to bed. Then I'd be up all night, twitching at the smallest sound outside. Lucas would be too, though he'd never admit it.

"Hey. You okay?"

I glance up to find Carson watching me. He looks concerned.

"I'm fine." I take another bite and chew slowly, thinking about Lucas again.

Some guy walks by with a beer in hand and trips over the log we're sitting on. He almost falls into the fire but Carson grabs him.

"Thanks, man," he slurs and stumbles away.

I wonder why Carson doesn't drink, but I'm reluctant to ask. I don't like to pry.

"You're wondering why I don't drink, right?"

I stare at him. "How did you know?"

"Lucky guess." He stares at the fire as he roasts another marshmallow for himself. "I got smashed at a party last summer and thought it would be a good idea to go surfing. At night." He shakes his head and rolls his eyes. "I almost drowned. I would have if someone hadn't seen me go under." He looks over at me and shrugs. "Haven't touched alcohol since."

I wouldn't either.

One of the girls from earlier plops down on the other side of Carson and slips her arm through his. "Hey, Carson. Everyone's going swimming. You comin'?"

He turns toward me and our eyes meet for a moment before he shakes his head. "I'm good."

She laughs and nudges him with her shoulder. "Still worried about your foot? Or is it something else?" She smiles at me, but it's anything but genuine.

"You can go," I say, getting to my feet. "I'd better get back anyway."

She smiles and I see her grip tighten on Carson's arm. He stands quickly and her arm slips through his. She follows his lead and folds her arms, looking disappointed. She doesn't take her eyes off me. They're curious and probing. I don't like it.

"You don't have to go, Oakley. I'm not going swimming. I'll just be supervising. I can use the company," Carson says.

I really want to say yes, but I can't get over how annoyed the girl looks, so I shake my head and give them my best smile. "Thanks, but I'm okay. Really. I'd better get back anyway. It's getting late." I glance at the girl. "It was nice to meet you."

"You too," she says sweetly.

"Thanks for the s'more, Carson. And for walking me over here."

I turn to leave and feel a hand on my shoulder. "I can walk you home," he says.

"It's okay. I don't want to keep you from your friends."

"Oakley." He looks disappointed and I feel bad, but it's really not a big deal.

"I'm right across the street. I'll be fine."

"She's right, Carson. She'll be fine." The girl grabs his arm and pulls him toward the water.

He shakes her off again and she folds her arms, waiting. Someone lets out a whoop and the sound of splashing fills the night. He glances behind him before looking at me again. "I really do want to walk you home, but I'm afraid I'm the designated lifeguard tonight." He looks behind him again, unease filling his features. "I don't want my friends getting into trouble. I probably shouldn't leave them."

"I totally understand." He still looks disappointed, but I smile to reassure him.

"Okay. Can I see you tomorrow?"

He really wants to see me again? "Yes," I say, a blush creeping in. I don't mean to blurt it, it just happens. "Bye, Carson."

"Be careful."

I don't answer, just nod and start back up the beach to Jo's house. As much as I want to turn around to see what exactly they're going to do, I don't. I just keep walking. Back to Mom, who I'm sure is still mad at me. Back to another restless night full of bad memories that are impossible to forget. Back to reality. And my pathetic little bubble I now call my life.

CHAPTER 5

The first thing I see the next morning is Lucas's notebook sitting on my bedside table. I grab for it and once it's in my hands, I flip to page three and read my daily entry.

DEAR OAKLEY,

 I KNOW THIS MAY COME AS A SHOCK, BUT ALL THOSE TIMES YOU'VE MADE ME WATCH THE VAMPIRE DIARIES WITH YOU? WELL, I SECRETLY LIKED IT . . .

 TELL ANYONE AND I'LL HAUNT YOU FOREVER. FOR REAL.

I laugh out loud. I swear he hated that show. Every time I turned it on, he complained. But I guess he *did* watch it with me every week. And now that I think about it, he would ask a lot of questions when it was on.

 AND PROMISE ME YOU WON'T BECOME ONE OF THOSE WEIRD FANGIRLS WHO CRY WHEN THEY SEE THE ACTORS ON TV AND STUFF. SERIOUSLY. YOU KNOW THE ONES I'M TALKING ABOUT . . .

MY ADVICE TODAY? GET OUT AND LEARN SOMETHING NEW. I'VE ALWAYS WANTED TO LEARN TO PLAY THE DRUMS. IS THAT RANDOM OR WHAT?

LOVE, LUCAS

I set the book aside and open the French doors, surprised to see clouds in the sky. I can smell the ocean mixed with rain. A smile creeps to my lips as the first drops start to fall. I hold my hand out and catch some of them in my palm. Rain always makes me happy—especially when it comes with lightning and thunder. I love a good storm.

I didn't always though. Every time a thunderstorm came around when I was little, I'd run to my parents room, terrified, but Mom and Dad would always tell me everything was fine and to go back to sleep. I'd go back to my room and curl in a ball until the storm ended.

One night, during a really loud storm, Lucas found me huddled at the top of my bed. Even though I was seven, I still remember every detail. He grabbed my hand and took me into his room. After tucking me into his bed, he sat in his window seat and told me hilarious made-up stories until the storm died down.

It was something he did more times than I can count. Even this last year at the hospital when a bad thunderstorm hit, I curled up next to him in his bed as he twisted a fairy tale around about how Snow White and Cinderella had to duke it out over the handsome prince. The story was full of professional wrestling moves, a few of the seven dwarfs tag-teaming Cinderella, and field mice biting Snow White's toes.

Even if his stories were bizarre, I could always count on him to make me laugh.

I take a deep breath before I step back inside and go find some breakfast.

Jo's in the kitchen, buttering a piece of toast. When she sees me, she grabs two cups and fills both with orange juice.

"Thanks," I say as she sets one on the counter in front of me. "Where's my mom?"

She shrugs. "She's already out and about. She said she had some things to do today and not to wait to eat."

"Oh." I frown. She usually tells me where she's going. Weird.

Jo's watching me, a look of concern mixed with sadness on her face. "You have fun last night?" she asks.

I shrug. "It was okay. Didn't really know anyone." Oh, and all the girls seem to hate me already. I decide not to mention that, though. I don't want her to try to make the girls be friends with me. It seems like something she would do.

She nods and takes a sip of juice. "Any plans today?"

"No." I grab a banana off the table and stick a piece of bread in the toaster. "Do you have any peanut butter?"

She laughs and shakes her head. "You're just like your mom." She gestures to the cupboard behind me. "She used to have it all the time when we were younger." She wrinkles her nose. "Never understood why she liked it. I like them separate, but together? That's nasty."

"It's the best," I say with a shrug.

As I make my peanut butter and bananas on toast, we're both quiet. Jo takes a seat and picks up the newspaper sitting on the table. She chews slowly while she reads.

I savor every bite of my toast. It reminds me of home.

"So, you really don't have plans?"

I look up and shake my head. "Why? What's up?"

"I was wondering if you wanted to come on the boat today. I'm going to check on some blue whales in Newport. They're always fun to watch."

"I'd love to!" I'm surprised at the excitement in my voice, but how could I not be excited to see real live whales?

"Great. Go get ready. Wear something light so you don't overheat out there. And don't forget sunscreen. With your light skin, you'll fry."

I shove the last bite of toast in my mouth and run to my room to change.

It takes fifteen minutes to drive to the harbor where Jo keeps her boat. There's a long pier to my left with rows of docks extending out into the water. I can't believe how many boats are tied to the docks. Too many to count.

I wonder how Jo can even find her boat, but she does. It's white and smallish but really nice.

"*Solo*?" I smile at the name etched on the side. "Is there a story behind this?"

She laughs. "I was gonna put Han on there first but then I wanted it to be more subtle."

"You're kidding."

"Hey, just because I'm a beach girl doesn't mean I can't like *Star Wars*."

I raise my hands in defense. "I wasn't making fun, I swear."

She chuckles. "You thought it. And please tell me you know who that is."

Of course I do. Who doesn't? "He shot first."

She rustles my hair with her hand. "That's my girl. Now hop inside. Let's get out of here."

I don't even hesitate before climbing aboard, careful to keep my camera away from any water. I wait for her to detach *Solo* from the dock and then we're off.

The sun is hot on my skin and it takes me a minute before I realize I forgot my sunscreen. Of course. Oh well. Hopefully Jo has some aloe for later.

The sky is still a little cloudy, but the water is calm and gorgeous as Jo sails us into the middle of nowhere. I admit I'm a little claustrophobic, or . . . I guess the opposite of claustrophobic, since I'm in a huge monster ocean with too much space. I pull out my cell, surprised to still have service, and look up the opposite of *claustrophobic* before I lose it. *Agoraphobic* pops up. Fear of open spaces? I think that works.

In spite of feeling really small and vulnerable in the huge ocean, it really is beautiful out here. Tranquil, peaceful. I could get used to this, I think. After I get over the whole agoraphobia thing. I lean against the side of the boat as my hair blows in the wind. Waves splash against the side and I feel a few drops on my arm.

"So, what kind of animals do you work with?" I ask Jo. I have to talk louder than normal since the boat engine is so loud. "You *do* work with animals, right?"

Jo looks back at me, the wind flying through her mess of curls. "I work with all kinds of sea mammals." She slows the boat down a little and looks back at me. "I work at the Save Sea Life rehabilitation center. We rescue injured and sick seals, sea lions, and cetaceans."

"Ceta-what?"

She must see the confusion on my face because she smiles. "Whales, dolphins, and porpoises."

"Oh. I didn't know they had a group name. For some reason I thought you swam with sharks and stuff. Or sat at a desk all day doing marine biology research."

She laughs. "Nope. Although, I've been swimming with sharks a few times."

"Was it scary?"

"Not really. I stayed pretty close to the surface and was very careful."

I shiver. You couldn't pay me a million dollars to do that. "So, what have you rescued lately?" I'm intrigued and impressed at how cool my aunt is for rescuing sea animals. Seriously. How many people can say that?

"Well, we rescued a few sea lions this month. And a dolphin that managed to beach herself. Our most interesting rescue was a baby gray whale a few years ago. We named her Mae. We searched the ocean for her mom for a few days, but never found her. Took us forever to beach her so we could get her the help she needed. I grew really attached to her. We had to transfer her to a different facility because of her size, so that was a hard day, but for the best. She's doing great now. We've seen her every year since we released her back into the ocean."

"Cool. Do you do anything else besides rescue?"

"We help make sure the mammals out in the ocean are thriving. Keep them safe from . . . well . . . us. Humans are the ultimate predator as far as sea life is concerned. Litter, oil spills. It's pretty bad."

I stare out into the water, thinking of all the problems the world has. The ocean, especially. I've seen some documentaries on oil spills and what it does to the animals who are unfortunate enough to get caught in them. Fish, whales, birds. It's awful. And then those fishing nets that strangle dolphins and other sea creatures is sad to think of too. I'm so proud of Jo for saving animals like that.

"Did you know blue whales are on the endangered species list?"

I shake my head. "I don't know a lot about them. All I know is that they're really, really big."

"Largest mammal on Earth." She looks around for a second and steers us to the right. We pass what looks like a tour boat full of people and she waves at the captain. She looks back at me. "People started hunting them in the 1800s, along with several other species, but the blue whales were the biggest prize, obviously. They're fast and tough to catch, but whalers got the best of them. They killed hundreds of thousands of blue whales for over a century, until the International Whale Commission finally banned whalers from killing any more of them in 1966. But of course there were still poachers for a few years after that. Even after people stopped killing them, their populations can't seem to recover. They're fascinating creatures. Intelligent, quick for their large size, and gentle. They're my favorite species of whale."

"I've never seen one up close, just pictures."

"I see the pod ahead." She slows the boat down right when I spot a whale poking its head out of the water. The blowhole sprays foam and water everywhere and I watch, transfixed, as it dives down again.

I grab my camera and take a few pictures. "They're amazing," I say as the tail splashes water into the boat.

"I know, right?" She turns off the motor of the boat and we sit and watch as several other whales break the surface. "I know they know I'm here but they've never bothered me. They just do their own thing."

A whale appears about a foot from our small boat and shoots water out of its blowhole. I shove my camera under my shirt as it rains down on us.

Jo reaches out a hand and touches its slick-looking skin. "You can touch him if you want. Since they're so big, it's easy to reach out and touch them before they go under again."

I don't hesitate at all and reach out to feel the cool, slippery skin. I slide my fingers over it and watch the droplets of water scatter across the dark surface. The whale moves underneath my hand, going slow but steady, until it disappears into the water again. "The skin is so weird. Cool, but weird."

"Their skin feels weird because the dead cells they shed actually adhere to the surface. That's what makes it slimy. It acts as a lubricant to allow them to move through the water more easily and reduce drag. The layer of fat underneath the skin is called blubber. It helps keep the whale warm. This water gets very cold and they have so much blubber they don't seem to feel it."

Jo is so smart. "Sweet."

Another whale appears on the other side of the boat and I watch, fascinated, as its long body moves past us and finally disappears under the water again. It's amazing how huge whales are. It's like nothing can hurt them. Besides poachers, I guess. As I watch a few more swim near the boat, I'm surprised I'm okay with them being so close. They could knock us out of the boat in seconds and eat us for dinner. But I know whales don't eat people. Well, besides Jonah, I guess. He had it coming though.

"You're getting a little red. You ready to head back?"

"Sure." I look at my arms, surprised to see a little pink tint to them. I didn't think we were out that long.

"You get more sun when you're surrounded by water," Jo explains. "And with your light skin, you don't stand a chance."

"I guess that makes sense."

"You forgot your sunscreen, didn't you?" She smirks at me.

"Uh . . ." I trail off and look back at the whales.

I hear her chuckle behind me. "I warned you. I have some aloe back at the house. The way you're already burning, you'll need it tonight."

I shrug. No big deal. It was totally worth it.

CHAPTER 6

On our way home, Jo picks up some McDonald's for the two of us. When we pull into the driveway a few minutes later, she grabs the bag of food and grins. "How about we have a picnic on the beach? I don't want to go inside yet."

"Sounds good," I say. "I need to run in and put on some sunscreen really quick. I'll grab a beach blanket while I'm in there."

"Okay. I'll wait for you out here."

I skip up the porch steps and go inside. As I pass Mom's room, I open her door to see if she's in there, but the room's empty. Where did she go? She doesn't know anyone around here, and why would she leave without telling me? I shake my head and go to my room, trying not to let it bother me. I grab some sunscreen off the desk and rub it on my arms, shoulders, and face before heading back outside with a blanket tucked under my arm.

Five minutes later, we're sitting a few yards from the waves, relaxing and enjoying our food.

"Do you do this a lot?" I ask as I shove my last fry in my mouth.

She shakes her head. "Not really. The last time I did this was with my ex-boyfriend." She chuckles. "I'd rather not talk about him though. He's old news."

"Oh. Okay." I'm kind of glad; something tells me Jo's love life is really complicated.

"Hey, Jo!" Someone calls from across the beach. We both look over and see Carson running toward us, carrying his surfboard. He's wet from head to toe and still has a slight limp, but he's obviously well enough to be surfing again.

"Carson, you better be taking care of that foot. You shouldn't be out surfing so soon."

He shrugs and his eyes shift to mine, but only for a second. "It's nothing. Good as new, in fact."

She frowns. "Just keep it wrapped up. You don't want to hurt it even more. And if you bleed, you know what you could attract."

"I know. No worries, Jo. I'm not even surfing; I'm teaching today." He smiles and looks at me. "Hey, Oakley. Nice to see you again."

"Hi." I refuse to look at Jo. I can feel her watching me and I pray she doesn't say anything to embarrass me.

"Well, just thought I'd say hi. I'd better get back. My student's waiting for me." He backs up, his eyes still on mine until he finally turns around and runs back into the water.

He gives surf lessons? Huh. As I watch him in the water, I think back on Lucas's advice for the day. *Learn something new.* What about surfing? Right. Like I could learn how to surf. Carson's probably been surfing since he was a little kid. I'm seventeen. I'm like that stupid saying: you can't teach an old dog new tricks.

But what if I *could* learn how to surf? I wonder what he charges? Maybe if I see him again I'll ask him about it. Learning something new could be good for me.

I can still feel Jo staring at me. I sneak a look at her and frown at the grin she's giving me. "He's a good guy. You really should go out with him."

I sigh. "He seems like he is, but I'm not really here to date people. I'm leaving in a few months anyway." I fold my arms and watch Carson in the water again. "Besides, he hasn't asked me out, so how could I go out with him?"

"Oh, I don't know. You could always ask *him.*"

I chuckle. "Can you really see me asking anyone out? I can't even look people in the eye when I talk to them."

Jo laughs. "You're not *that* shy."

"I am. There's no way I could get up the guts to ask a guy out. Especially one I barely know. And isn't it the guy's job to ask the girl out?"

"It's the twenty-first century, babe. Girls ask guys out all the time now."

"I know. I just . . . can't. It would be weird."

"Too bad for you." She stands, grabs the wrappers from our dinner, and starts back toward the house. I watch Carson standing on the beach, talking to a boy who looks like he's about eight. He says something and points to the waves, ruffles the kid's hair, and walks out in the water with him.

He looks so at ease. Relaxed. Cute.

I shake my head. Stupid. I don't need a guy to distract me. I'm trying to find myself. Or move on or whatever. Start over. I take one last look at him before following Jo back to the house.

I'm surprised to see Mom when we walk back in. She's on the phone and looks like she hasn't slept in days. She sees me, stops talking, and gives me a small smile. I'm sure it's Dad on the other end but I don't stick around long enough to find out. Even though I want to know where she's been all day, I don't want to know what's going on between them. Not now, anyway. By the way Mom looks, it's not good.

I head to my room, change out of my sweaty tank top and shorts, and put on a yellow sundress. I'm not a huge fan of dresses, but I like the happy color. And it's freaking hot outside, so it feels nice to wear something light. I put more sunscreen on my arms and face, grab my camera, and head across the street to the beach. I don't really have a plan for where I'm going but end up at the tide pools again.

Once there, I take a few more photographs of the rocks, the ocean, and the starfish. The starfish are still close to the surface and this time I don't hesitate at all as I set my camera on the rock and reach my hand into the cold water to grab one. I cringe a little as I pull it away from the rock it's stuck to and turn it over to see the little sucker things on the other side. I wonder if the little hole in the center of the starfish is the mouth? I'm not really an expert on starfish anatomy, so I have no idea. I may have to look it up when I get home.

"You really like those starfish."

I jump and curse as I almost knock my camera into the water.

"Sorry," Carson said. "I always seem to scare you."

"Yeah, you kind of have a habit of showing up out of nowhere." I smile and scoot back from the water, making sure my dress is down. I didn't realize how unladylike I was sitting before he showed up. Hopefully he didn't notice. "And yes, I do like starfish. They're pretty cool. Not as cool as whales, but they're still interesting."

"Whales are amazing."

"They really are. Jo took me out on the boat earlier and showed me a bunch of blue whales. In person! It was awesome."

He nods. "Your aunt's the coolest. Mind if I sit?" He gestures to the rock beside me.

I smile up at him. "I'd love some company." As the words come out, I realize how true they are.

He sits down and leans back on his hands, totally relaxed. There are drops of water in his light hair and he runs his hand through it to get them out. He's still in his wet suit, though he's pulled the top down so it hangs low around his waist. I can't help but peek at his ripped chest. It's nice. Nice enough for me to stare at him like an idiot. Which I'm still doing.

"Do you like being by yourself all the time?"

His question catches me off guard and I look away from his body and out into the water. "No, not really." I hate it, especially since I used to spend all my time with Lucas at the hospital. I don't want to admit I'm lonely, but that's the only word that comes to mind. "I just don't really know anyone around here, so I don't really have a choice."

"Then you should hang out with us." He sets his hand on my shoulder and squeezes it before leaning back again.

I give him a small smile. "I'm pretty sure those girls you introduced me to last night don't like me much."

He gives me a weird look and shakes his head. "They're just girls. Shy until they get to know someone." His shoulder bumps mine. "Kind of like you, I think."

"I guess." I realize I'm still holding the starfish.

"Just drop it in the water and it will eventually get back to the rock by itself. Try not to drop it on its back or it'll get stuck."

"I rescued a starfish that was stuck on its back yesterday," I tell him. I lean over the tide pool, drop it, and watch it until it lands at the bottom. I wonder if it's cursing me for making it have to climb all the way up the rocks again.

"Perfect," he says.

I lean back and don't realize how close he is until I turn to look at him. His face is inches from mine and his brown eyes are light and curious. His breath catches and his eyes flick to my lips. My heart races and I realize

I haven't moved. What am I doing? I'm supposed to be grieving. Not lusting after some guy.

Embarrassed and mad at myself, I move over a little and stretch my legs in front of me. He follows suit, his legs stretched out a few inches from mine. We sit there for a while, not saying much. I can't really look at him anyway, since that moment was sort of awkward. Instead I pass the time taking pictures of the surfers on the water while he points out different creatures in the tide pools.

I gasp when I see a guy on his board crash pretty hard on a wave, but he comes up sputtering and goes right back out for another run. "I don't know how you guys do that."

Carson looks up. "Surf?"

I nod. "It looks so hard. And when the wave pushes you under the water . . ." I rub the goosebumps on my arms and shake my head.

"It's not too bad. Once you get up the first time, it gets easier."

"I doubt that." I watch the same guy fall again. That would be me. No . . . I would have fallen off a lot sooner than he did.

"I can teach you if you're interested in learning."

My heart races. "Really?" I look at him, but he doesn't notice. He's staring out into the waves again.

"Of course. It would be my pleasure." He glances at me for a second and looks away again.

I put my camera away. *Learn something new.* Part of me is terrified and the other part is thrilled. It would definitely take my mind off things. And having a hot surfer teach me wouldn't be so bad either. I lean toward him. "Could we start tomorrow?" I smile and blush at how forward I sound. "I mean—"

"I'll tell you what. If you let me show you around the city tonight, I'll start our lessons tomorrow."

"Why do you want to show me around?"

He shrugs and plays with a brown bracelet around his wrist, not meeting my eyes. "I like going into town and you're new and should see what's around. And it would be nice to have a pretty girl on my arm."

I laugh. He sounds like he's from a different century.

"That sounded really lame, right?" He laughs too. "I was trying to be polite, not weird. I'm serious though. I'd like some company and who better than you?"

"Oh." This time I swear my whole body turns red. I'm flattered he thinks I'm interesting enough to hang out with, but not quite sure what to say. I didn't come here looking for a relationship . . . but honestly, I really could use a friend.

"So, will you come?"

I glance at him and try not to get lost in his brown-eyed gaze. Which is surprisingly hard. "Sure. What time?"

He stands and I grab my camera as he takes my hand and helps me up. "How about six? We can grab some dinner and I'll show you around the pier."

"Okay."

"Mind if I walk you back to your place?"

I shake my head. "Not at all."

He helps me down from the rocks and grabs his surfboard which has been lying on the sand. I didn't even notice it before. It's yellow. Almost the same color as my dress. He holds it under one arm and I can't help but stare at him again.

"Get any good pictures today?"

"A few."

"You'll have to show me some of them. Sometime . . ." He trails off and smiles at the look on my face. "What?"

I wring my hands together and chew on my lip. "I don't know. I don't really show a lot of people my work."

"Well, you should. I can tell you love it. Taking pictures, I mean."

"It's fun. Therapeutic, I guess."

"Therapeutic?"

I stop walking for a second and clear my throat. "Um . . . never mind." I'm not going there.

Thankfully, he leaves it alone.

We reach the house sooner than I want. It's nice hanging out with someone close to my age.

"I'll see you tonight then?"

"Yes. Thanks for walking me back."

He pats me on the back and his hand lingers a little longer than it should. "No problem."

I say goodbye and walk inside, shutting the door behind me. I'm not sure what to think about this. Am I doing the right thing? Mom told me to make friends, but me and a guy alone together? I'm not sure that's what she meant. Even so, he said he'd teach me how to surf. And Lucas would be proud of me for learning something new. So, the main reason I'm going with Carson is because I want to thank him for volunteering to teach me to surf. Yes. That's it. It's not a date; it's not a romantic stroll on the pier. It's business only.

With that thought, I head to my room and stare at the pile of clothes heaped in my closet. What am I going to wear tonight?

CHAPTER 7

I'm addicted to Lucas's random thoughts. Before I start stressing out about Carson, I read an entry in the notebook. His words are calming. I know I should wait and save one for each day, but I need to read what he has to say next.

DEAR OAKLEY,

YOU KNOW HOW I LIKE TO SING IN THE SHOWER AT HOME? I TOTALLY DO IT HERE, TOO. A KID ON MY FLOOR SAYS I HAVE A PRETTY AWESOME VOICE. HE EVEN GAVE ME A RECOMMENDATION TO SING TOMORROW. I THINK IT'S HILARIOUS THAT HE CAN HEAR ME, SINCE HE'S ALL THE WAY DOWN THE HALL. THAT MEANS I'M LOUDER THAN I THOUGHT I WAS. MAYBE I'LL TONE IT DOWN A LITTLE . . .

NAH. I'M GOOD.

I WOULD ASK YOU TO SING A DUET, BUT YOU KNOW . . . HA HA.

LOVE, LUCAS

Did he have to bring up my crappy singing voice again? With a smile on my face, I close the notebook and go get ready.

Carson picks me up at six. When I open the front door, he stares at me and clears his throat. "You look amazing."

"Thanks." I wouldn't say *amazing*, but I did put on a little more makeup and actually thought about what to wear. Which, since this was just a business outing, made no sense at all. I look down at my light blue tank and my favorite jeans and blush. They're not the nicest but I have to admit, the jeans make my butt look pretty good. At least that's what my friends used to tell me.

"Hey, Carson." Jo peeks around the corner and waves.

"Hey, Jo! Do you need my help anytime soon?"

"I'm sure I could use you this week. Just stop in anytime." She smiles and leaves us alone.

I don't say goodbye to Mom. I haven't seen her since earlier. Maybe tomorrow I'll ask her about her phone conversation with Dad and why she looks so tired all the time, but for now, I'm going to enjoy myself.

"You ready?" Carson asks.

"Yep." My palms are sweaty and I'm sure my armpits are, too. How embarrassing. I should have worn a darker shirt.

Carson seems at ease as he walks me to his Jeep. I stare at the beast in front of me. I've never ridden in a Jeep before. It's green and black and I'm sure really windy. I'm glad my hair is in a ponytail. He opens the passenger door for me and I climb in with trembling hands.

"This is nice," I say as he climbs in the driver's seat and starts it up.

"Thanks. She's my baby. I named her Helga."

Helga? I think it's kind of goofy when guys name their cars, but I decide to keep that thought to myself.

We sit in silence as he drives down the street. I'm not sure what to say, how to act. I have no idea where to put my hands, so I keep them in my lap. I want to fold my arms, but figure I'd look uncomfortable or cold or something when I'm boiling hot. Still sweating, actually. Good times.

I don't know where he's taking me or what we're going to do, I'm just glad to be out of the house with another person. And as a bonus, a really attractive and nice person.

After a few minutes of driving, he pulls into a parking lot. A bunch of cute shops line the street and he parks in front of a surfing one called Nye's Surf Shop. He gets out and I do the same. I'm not about to make him walk around to open the door for me, which by the look on his face, he was clearly coming to do. I smile and shrug.

This isn't a date. I have to keep reminding myself of that fact.

The air is warm and a slight breeze tousles my hair. I cross my arms and join Carson as we walk toward the shop together.

A white sign with bright blue paint sits next to the door. SURFING LESSONS AVAILABLE. DETAILS INSIDE.

I'm curious if Carson is going to get someone from this shop to teach me how to surf instead of giving me lessons himself. Before I can ask, he pulls the screen door open and a little bell jingles. He waits until I walk inside and lets the door shut behind him.

The shop is amazing. Surfboards are everywhere in every color you can imagine. They hang on wires attached to the ceiling, are stacked neatly against the wall, and a few are actually hung on the wall. I'm not sure if they're decorations or if they are actually available for purchase.

I notice a price tag on one and get my answer.

There are shirts, wet suits, board shorts, and tank tops hung on the racks throughout the store. Hats, sunglasses, and other little things are on displays as well. I see a cute pair of pink board shorts and stop myself from checking the price on them. I'm not here to shop, but if I were, I'd totally buy them.

"Hey, Dillon," Carson says.

I look up to see Dillon waiting at the counter. He's rubbing something on an orange surfboard and when he sees me, he breaks into a smile.

I take a step forward so I'm standing by Carson. It smells like coconuts and I'm not sure if it's Dillon or the surfboard.

"Oakley," he says, taking a pair of sunglasses off his head and pointing at its logo. He laughs.

Like I haven't heard that one before. I smile anyway.

"What brings you two here?" He glances curiously at Carson.

"Just taking Oakley out to see the pier."

So that's where we're going. Huntington Pier. I've heard of it, but obviously haven't been.

Dillon shoots Carson a look I can't read. "Really? It's pretty cool."

"I'm taking her on a bike ride first."

What? Is he joking?

"Why didn't you just ride your bikes instead of drive?"

"Because my bike is *here*. And so is Keilani's. Oakley's going to borrow hers. She won't mind."

Dillon laughs. "That's what you think. She'll kick your butt if she finds out."

Carson shrugs. "I can take her."

I stare at both of them with wide eyes. He would beat up a girl over a bike? He must be joking.

"I get off in an hour or so. Maybe I'll join ya," Dillon says.

Carson glances at me and hesitates before nodding. "Sure."

"We can show Oakley how to have a good time." He smiles. "There's tons of stuff to do around here."

"Sounds like a party," I say. Dillon raises an eyebrow and gives me a wicked grin, which confirms I've said the wrong thing.

Carson clears his throat next to me. "You ready?"

"Sure." But I'm really not. I haven't ridden a bike in years and I'm pretty sure it's going to be a disaster. Actually, I'm positive it will be.

"See you later, Dill," Carson says.

I feel Dillon's eyes on me as I follow Carson to the back of the store.

He leads me through a doorway with beads hanging down to the ground, past a bunch of surfboards and a pile of boxes, and finally to the very back of the store. Several bikes lean against the wall and he points at a light blue one and hands me a helmet. "You can ride this one."

I stare at him, the helmet in my hand.

"What?" he asks. "You know how to ride a bike?"

"Well, yes, but—"

"Then you'll be fine." He smiles and opens the back door. It's getting dark but there are streetlights everywhere. He walks his bike out to the boardwalk. Lots of people are out even though it's almost sunset. How would it be to live in a place like this forever? I don't think I'd mind it.

"This is the boardwalk, which I'm sure you already know. It's the same boardwalk across the street from your aunt's house, but we're about six miles away. It stretches from Sunset Beach, goes through Huntington Beach for about nine miles, and then you can go three or so more miles until you hit Newport Peninsula. It's a great workout if you're into that sort of thing."

I nod. "Cool."

"The pier's right there. Past all those shops."

I look where he's pointing. There're a bunch of shoppers and I'm pretty sure I'm going to kill someone.

"That's where we're going." He smiles and puts his helmet on. "Don't run anyone over, okay?" He grins and gets on his bike.

"I'll try not to." I feel really self-conscious but put my helmet on and swing my leg over the seat of my borrowed bike anyway. It's a little big and my toes barely touch the ground. Carson stands up on his pedals and bounces next to me. He's obviously a biker. My friend Emmy back home would get along great with him. I watch him bounce a few more times until he notices the look on my face and laughs.

"Don't worry. I'll stay with you."

Not very reassuring, but I smile and pretend my heart's not beating a million miles an hour. I push off the ground and while I'm a little wobbly at first, my feet find the pedals and we're off.

We pass a lot of people, most with shopping bags, and they're all super friendly. A lot of them have dogs and I try to maneuver my bike as far away as possible so I don't hit one or get chased.

I swear it takes forever to reach the pier but it's probably only been five minutes. I'm sweating and a little out of breath, which is ridiculous. We didn't even go that far.

Carson jumps off his bike and wheels it over to a bike rail, pulls out two locks, and puts one of them on his bike. I wobble as I put my feet down to stop. My toes scrape the ground and I'm grateful I have real shoes on instead of flip-flops. That would have been a mess.

"Here," he says, locking my bike next to his. He steps back and takes in a deep breath. "Let's go get something to eat."

People are everywhere. A lot of women wearing string bikini tops and short shorts. A few guys stand in front of a bar, tattoos covering half their torsos and arms, holding drinks and look like they're having a good time. We pass a guy playing some little drums and another guy probably in his twenties singing while playing his guitar.

I take it all in since it's nothing like back home. I know my parents sheltered me and it probably shows.

Carson stops at a hot dog stand. "Best hot dogs you'll ever taste," he says. "I figured I could show you around more if we got hot dogs. I'm going to have to take you to Ruby's one of these days." He gestures to a building with a red roof at the end of the pier.

I smile. "That would be cool."

He walks up to the window and orders two hot dogs, then turns back to me. "What would you like on yours?"

"A little bit of ketchup and a lot of mustard."

A few minutes later, we're walking down the board-walk, hot dogs in hand. And Carson wasn't lying. It really is the best hot dog I've tasted.

"Mustard, huh? I'm more of a ketchup kind of guy. And relish."

I wrinkle my nose. "I'm not a fan of relish. Or pickles.

69

Though I do like the smell of them. Which I'm aware is weird."

He laughs and throws his wrapper in a garbage can. "You're funny."

I take one more bite and throw my wrapper away as well.

We keep walking.

"So, what do you like to do? I mean . . . do you have any hobbies or anything? Besides photography?"

"Not really." I hesitate. "I play the guitar a little, but other than that—"

"Seriously? I've always wanted to play the guitar." He shoves his hands in his pockets and looks at the ground as we walk. "I'm not very musically inclined." He catches my stare out of the corner of his eye and grins.

I feel my cheeks heat and clear my throat. I realize I'm twisting my ring around my finger and stop. Why am I so nervous around him? It's not like we're on a date or anything. "I'm not that musical either. My mom made me take piano lessons when I was little, but I hated them. She insisted I learn at least one instrument, or sing, which I'll never do in front of anyone."

He throws back his head and laughs. He has a nice laugh. Not weird or annoying, like some guys I know. Just . . . nice. "You mean you didn't get roped into taking choir in school?"

"They would have kicked me out. I suck." And it's the truth. Lucas never let me forget it. I take after my dad—totally tone deaf.

"I don't believe it."

"You should. I wish I could sing, but I just can't. So, instead of making a fool out of myself, I decided to take guitar lessons." I shrug. "I want to learn how to play the drums someday, but I doubt that will ever happen. I like the guitar though."

"You'll have to play for me sometime."

Not likely. "Maybe," I say.

"Or you could teach me." He nudges me with his shoulder. "Guitar lessons for surf lessons? What do you think?"

I stop walking and stare at him. He looks hopeful. "Are you serious?"

He shrugs. "I think it's an even trade, don't you?"

I'm not sure *what* to say. That means we'll be spending even more time together. I don't know how I feel about that. Although, he *is* super nice. And he smells good. And he's nice to look at . . . not that I noticed. "Sure," I say.

We both smile and I try not to feel nervous again. But the way he's looking at me makes me feel . . . weird instead. But a good weird. Which is bad news.

He finally looks away and clears his throat. "Looks like Ruby's is busy tonight." He gestures toward the restaurant on the end of the pier. Several people stand around outside. I watch a redheaded girl about my age snuggle against her boyfriend as they wait in line. He nuzzles her neck and she giggles before turning around and kissing him. They look so happy. Like nothing in the world would ever tear them apart.

I envy them. Not because they're in love, but because they have each other. They have someone to laugh with.

71

To hang out with. I think of Lucas and my mood drops. The world sucks.

"You okay?"

I look up at Carson and put on a smile. "Fine."

We walk to the edge of the pier and lean against the railing. The sun reflects off the water as it sets. Reds, oranges, and yellows. It's so bright, it's almost blinding, but I can't tear my eyes away.

"It's beautiful here." I breathe in the salty air and sigh. I wish Lucas were here. He'd love the beach. There I go again. Thinking about him. Again. I turn my attention back to Carson, determined to block my depressing thoughts.

He's staring at the ocean with a small smile on his face. "I wouldn't want to live anywhere else. It's home."

"I'd love to live on the beach. It's so peaceful. And there's so much to do here. Swim and surf, go boating. I'd love to have somewhere to run or ride my bike with a view like this. Not that I really rode my bike back home. I had a friend who was really into mountain biking, but I could never get into it. To be honest, the thought of flying down a mountain covered in rocks and dirt terrified me. If I could have ridden on solid blacktop right next to a beach though, I would have."

"It really is nice most of the time," he said. "The storms can be pretty crappy, though." He rolls his shoulders and leans forward, resting his arms on the railing. "So, you're just here for a few months then?"

I sigh. "Yes. My mom . . . uh . . . we're here on an extended vacation. Just until summer."

I wait for him to ask why, but he doesn't. Which makes me like him even more. He respects my privacy, even though I know he can tell I'm hiding something. And I'm not really. I just don't want to talk about me or Lucas or my parents and whatever's going on with them.

"So, about those guitar lessons."

I smile. I can't help it. He seems to know when I need something light to talk about. It's almost like he can read my moods. It reminds me of Lucas. He always knew my moods, even better than I knew them myself. "You're really serious about those?"

"Of course!"

"I'm not very good."

"You wouldn't agree to teach me if you weren't that good."

I laugh. "I haven't agreed to anything yet."

"We'll see about that."

An arm wraps around my shoulder then and I'm suddenly being squeezed into someone's armpit. I didn't realize how sore my shoulders are from my sunburn until now. They hurt like crap. I try to wiggle away.

"Hey, guys!"

It's Dillon. I smile as he adjusts his arm, but he doesn't let go of me. "Hey," I say. It smells like coconut again, just like in the surf shop. So it was him! Are guys supposed to smell like that? I think of my coconut lotion at home and picture him slathering it on his arms and legs. He doesn't seem the type.

Carson glances at us for a second and looks back at the ocean. "Close up shop?"

Dillon laughs and punches him in the arm. "Of course. No worries, bro."

"Thanks. Get a lot of people in today?"

"Earlier. Not much tonight. A few people picking up their boards, but not much else. It's a Friday night. You know how Friday nights go. It'll be slammed tomorrow."

Carson nods. "Who works tomorrow?"

"Me and Keilani bright and early. You and your dad have the afternoon shift."

He groans. "Great."

I'm surprised by his reaction. I'm not the only one with parental problems?

"You can at least hit the waves in the morning," Dillan says. "I wish I could."

Carson just shrugs. "You and Keilani can go later. I'm sure she'd love to kick your butt."

Dillon frowns. "Dude. You don't have to rub it in."

Carson laughs. "Yes. I do."

I wonder who Keilani is. I glance at Carson, very aware that Dillon's arm is still around my shoulder. My skin is on fire. I'll have to remember to put aloe on when I get home. "So, you work at that surf shop too, Carson?"

Dillon chuckles. "He doesn't just work there. He owns it."

My mouth drops open. "Really?" I should have remembered Carson's last name was Nye, but obviously I didn't.

"It's my dad's shop but he lets me run it." He shrugs. "It's not a big deal."

"Whatever," Dillon says. "It's the best surf shop around.

With affordable and professional surfing lessons provided by Carson and yours truly. Tourists come from miles around to learn from us. Ask anyone."

I swear Carson blushes, but he doesn't disagree. He meets my eyes. "Are you ready to go or do you want to stay for a while?"

"I should probably be getting home. I haven't really seen my mom all day." I think about riding the bike again and try not to look worried. Riding a bike during the day is one thing. Riding one in the dark . . .

"Oh, come on, you two, I just got here. Let's hang out for a while," Dillon says.

"She's right, Dill. I don't want Jo to beat me up if I don't get her back at a decent hour." He smiles. "Because honestly? She could totally take me."

Dillon snorts. "Fine. I'm sticking around here, though." He squeezes my shoulder and even though he didn't do it hard, my sunburn stings and I wince. "See you two later."

"Sunburn?" Carson asks as we walk back down the pier.

I glance over at him, surprised. "How did you know?"

"You looked like you were in pain when he squeezed your shoulder. And your face is kind of red."

I stop and touch my face. "How red?"

He smiles and reaches out, brushing his knuckles lightly across my cheek. "Don't worry. Red looks good on you." He pulls his hand back, his eyes on mine.

The skin on my cheek tingles where he touched and I let out the breath I didn't know I was holding. *Say something. Say something.* "So . . . uh . . . should we keep walking? It's getting kind of late." I'm tongue-tied. I don't even know what I'm saying.

And it's not even that late.

He searches my face one more time before clearing his throat. "Yeah."

I try to ignore my thumping heart as we continue our walk back to the bikes, but as I glance over, one tiny smile from him makes it speed up again.

No one's ever looked at me like that before.

The ride back to the surf shop is uneventful. Except for almost running over a dog, I do pretty well.

Carson locks the bikes back in the store and we make our way to his Jeep and head home. We're both silent, each lost in our own thoughts. I try to keep my eyes on the road but end up glancing at him every now and then. We're so different. He's kind and funny and everyone seems to like him. I wish I could be that comfortable around people. It occurs to me, not for the first time, that maybe I can be if I learn to let more people in.

He hums along with the radio as he drives and glances over at me with a small smile. I want to be that carefree and happy too.

Is it possible to find happiness when it feels like you've lost not only yourself but everyone you love? They're all lost to me in some way, whether they're here or in heaven. Mom and Dad, my friends, Lucas. A breeze touches my skin and I shiver as I stare out the window.

"Here. Put this on." I feel something fall in my lap. A blanket. I don't realize how cold I am until I feel the warmth through my jeans. I look over at Carson and he shrugs. "It gets a little cold at night. Especially in this thing."

I pull the blanket up and smile. Seriously, can he be any nicer?

"I'm going to park at my house, if that's all right?"

I nod. It's next door, so it's not a big deal if I have to walk home.

We pull into his driveway a few minutes later. He stops the car and jumps out. I reach to open my own door, but he's already there, holding it open for me. He reaches out a hand and helps me down from the Jeep.

His hand is warm, and even though both my feet are firmly on the ground, he doesn't let go.

"Thanks," I say, slowly pulling my hand away, "for showing me around today."

"Can I walk you to your door?" He smiles as I stare at him and raises an eyebrow. "What?"

"Was this a date?" I ask.

He shrugs. "I don't know. Do you want it to be a date?"

"Uh . . . I'm not . . . do I?" My heart speeds up again. What *do* I want it to be?

"I think we should call it a date."

"Okay . . ."

He chuckles at my terrified expression. "May I walk you to the door then?" He holds out his elbow and I hesitate only a second before taking it.

"Yes, you may. Thanks." I hope he can't feel my body shaking. I'm so nervous.

The night is quiet as we walk up the driveway, so I try to think of something to fill the silence. "So . . . how did you get to be such a gentleman?"

"What do you mean?"

"Opening doors, walking me to the porch. Totally gentlemanly."

He shrugs. "My mom."

"I love her already."

"Most people do." He chuckles. "And she taught me well."

"Obviously. Tell her thanks for that."

We reach the porch and walk up the stairs, my heart beating a million miles an hour. I've never been good at doorstep scenes. Or whatever you want to call them. I never know what to say, or what to do, or . . . you know, if I'm supposed to let them hug or kiss me goodnight.

I feel my cheeks heat at the thought of kissing him. He wouldn't do that on the first date, would he? Not that it would be a bad thing . . . but still. A little fast, I think. For me at least.

"This was fun," he says as I let go of his elbow. "We should do it again sometime."

"It *was* fun." We both stand near the door, and I'm really not sure what to do at this part. "Thank you for taking me."

"You're welcome. Thanks for coming."

I glance up at him and we stare at each other for a

second, each not knowing what to say. Or at least, I don't know what to say. Or do. His gaze doesn't flinch away until I see it flicker to my lips. My breath catches and I step back, faster than I realize, and almost fall off the porch.·

"You okay?" he asks. There's a glimmer of something in his eye, like he's trying not to laugh.

"Yes. Fine." *Fine.* That stupid word again. I look at the door and back at him. Pretty sure it's time for me to go inside. "Um . . . goodnight?" I smile at my awkwardness, turn away and try to open the door, but it's locked and I end up smacking my face into it.

"Forget your key?" he asks with a chuckle.

I rub my forehead and frown. "Yeah . . . please tell me you didn't see that, even though I know you did." Someone just kill me. Please.

"Didn't see a thing."

"That's a relief." We stare at each other and before I know it, I giggle, snort, and burst out laughing at how ridiculous I'm being. *Holy awkward.* If anyone wins the prize, it would be me.

"You just snorted," he laughs.

"Pretty sure that was your imagination."

"Right!" He laughs again, deep and loud.

The door opens a second later and Jo peeks her head outside. "Oakley?"

"Hey, Jo," I say. "You locked me out."

"I thought you had a key?"

I shake my head, my eyes on Carson. I shoot him a smile and he smiles back. I'm not sure what to think about the way he's looking at me. Like he isn't sure what to think, either, but kind of likes it? I may be way off but at least he's still smiling and not running away. That's a good sign, I think.

"Thanks for dinner," I manage. "I'll see you. Sometime." I wish I could stop talking.

"Tomorrow morning," he says. "Remember? I'll pick you up at eight."

"For what?"

"Your first surf lesson." He grins and nods to Jo, who has her arm around me now.

"Oh yeah . . ." Jo's grip tightens on me and I cringe as my sunburn throbs. I'm *so* going to peel. "See you tomorrow then."

"Have a good night, ladies." He turns, hops off the porch, and takes off across the sand to his house, whistling as he goes.

I stare after him, not sure what to make of him. Or anything, really.

"I wish a guy would look at *me* that way," Jo says.

I glance at her and frown. "He wasn't looking at me like anything."

She snorts. "Sure."

CHAPTER 8

For the first time in weeks, I actually set my alarm. I don't push snooze when it goes off, and don't lie in bed all morning, like I've done the past month. And after looking at the clock, I'm proud to say it's not even eight yet.

Lucas's notebook sits on my nightstand and I reach over and grab it. His letters are part of my daily routine now. I love reading them and find myself anxiously waiting for what he has to say each morning.

DEAR OAKLEY,

YOU KNOW WHAT I WISH I WOULD HAVE DONE LAST YEAR IN HIGH SCHOOL? I'M SURE YOU'LL NEVER GUESS, SO HERE'S A SHOCKING TRUTH FROM YOUR TOO-COOL-FOR-SCHOOL BROTHER. HA HA. I'M SO LAME. ANYWAY, I WISH I WOULD HAVE TRIED OUT FOR THE MUSICAL. AND NO, I'M NOT JOKING. YOU OF ALL PEOPLE KNOW I CAN SING. AND APPARENTLY THE WHOLE SECOND FLOOR OF THE HOSPITAL DOES AS WELL. ANYWAY, ME IN A MUSICAL WOULD HAVE BEEN EPIC. AND IT WOULD HAVE BEEN A BONUS BECAUSE EMMY WAS IN IT. MAYBE I COULD HAVE ACTUALLY GOTTEN TO PLAY OPPOSITE OF HER.

I smile at the thought of the girl Lucas had a crush on for years. One of my best friends and neighbor, Emmy Martin. He never did tell her. Not that I know of anyway. He always dated other girls. Mainly stupid ones who didn't treat him well.

NOW, WITH THAT BEING SAID, I WANT YOU TO DO SOMETHING FOR ME. I'M ABOUT TO GO ALL PHILOSOPHICAL AGAIN, SO WATCH OUT. DON'T EVER LET THE FEAR OF WHAT OTHER PEOPLE MAY THINK OF YOU STOP YOU FROM PURSUING THE THING THAT MIGHT MAKE YOU GREAT.

I WISH I WOULD HAVE DONE MORE. I REGRET NOT TRYING OUT FOR THAT STUPID PLAY. ALL BECAUSE I THOUGHT THE BASKETBALL TEAM WOULD MAKE FUN OF ME. I DON'T KNOW WHY I LET THEM STOP ME. I COULD HAVE TAKEN ANY OF THEM IN A FIGHT ANYWAY. PROMISE ME YOU WON'T DO THE SAME THING I DID. LIVE YOUR LIFE. GO AFTER YOUR DREAMS. DON'T HAVE ANY REGRETS. AND MOST OF ALL, BE HAPPY.

LOVE, LUCAS

Go after your dreams. I let that sink in a moment, but I don't even know what my dreams are. What do I want? Where do I want to be in five years? I honestly have no idea, but I need to start thinking about it.

My thoughts turn back to Emmy. I should have talked to her before I left. We made so many memories together and when Lucas got diagnosed, I just shut her out. I feel awful about it. She didn't deserve to be treated like that, no matter how hard it was for me to deal with things. I should pick up the phone and call her but I can't do it. I wouldn't know what to say or where to begin with my apologies. I hope she's forgiven me, and if she hasn't, I know I'll apologize someday.

With those thoughts fresh in my mind, I get out of bed and change into my swimsuit, hoping I won't make a fool of myself today. Not that Carson won't be a good teacher—I'm sure he will—I just hope I won't let him down. Or myself down.

As soon as I'm done changing, the doorbell rings. I grab an elastic off my dresser and pull my hair in a quick bun to keep it out of my face while I surf. Or try to surf. I sigh. What am I getting myself into?

"Oakley," Jo yells down the hall, "you're wanted at the door!"

"Be there in a sec!" I yell back. I run across the hall to the bathroom to look at my reflection in the mirror and cringe at the turquoise swimsuit I'm wearing. It's not horrible, but not that flattering either. My hips are wider than I'd like, so I stay far away from bikinis. I'm sure I'll look plain and boring in a one-piece, but I don't care . . . much. If I'm going to be in a swimsuit, I need to wear the one that will make me the least uncomfortable.

I hurry and rub some aloe on my sunburned face and shoulders and put sunscreen on over that. Ready or not, I grab my towel and head to the door. Mom is in the kitchen. She looks exhausted. Her eyes have dark circles underneath and her hair's a mess. She doesn't notice me, but watches Jo talk quietly to Carson by the front door. When he sees me, his face breaks out into a wide grin. "You ready?"

"I hope so," I say. No. Not ready at all.

"See ya later, Jo." He looks past me and smiles at Mom, who's sitting at the table with a crooked smile on her face. "It's nice to meet you, Mrs. Nelson."

"Bye, Mom," I say.

She gives me a curious look but doesn't ask questions. She hesitates for a second before lifting her hand to wave. "Be careful."

"I'll be back soon." I'm not sure what else to say to her, so I follow Carson out the door. I know Mom and I should probably talk about things but I'm not going to be the one to bring anything up. She's the mom. If she wants to talk, then she needs to be the one to come to me. I'm not supposed to take care of her . . . right?

We step on the porch and Carson picks up his yellow surfboard. Besides a white line running down the middle and some logo at the top, it's pretty plain. He gestures to the side of me and I notice a board lying in the sand. It's white, save for a little blue line that goes vertically up the middle, and two pink flowers on either side of it.

"It's yours."

"What?" I stare at it and crouch down, running my fingers over it. It's kind of soft. "It's mine? Really?"

He shrugs and gives me half a smile. "It's a foam board. A little more squishy than others. You'll have an easier time learning on that, I think."

"You didn't need to buy me a surfboard," I say, standing up and folding my arms. I frown.

"It's not a big deal. I own a surf shop, remember?" He glances at the board. "Besides, it's used. If that makes you feel any better."

It doesn't look used at all. I don't know what to say. I'm sure surfboards are a lot of money but I don't dare ask him how much. He probably wouldn't tell me anyway.

"Oakley." I look up at him and he smiles. "I promise. It's okay." His fingers skim my arm before he leans down to pick up my board.

"Thank you," I whisper. "You really didn't need to buy me one."

"I know," he says, like it's no big deal. He pulls the board up and stands it next to me. "You ready?"

I stare at it and grimace. It's huge. Way taller than me. If he let go of it, it would smash me into the ground. I grab the side of it and smile at him. "So, how the heck am I going to get this all the way across the street and down to the beach?"

He laughs. "It's not too heavy. And if it does get too heavy, you can drag it. Just not on the road." He leans down and picks up two wet suits and towels that sit on the ground beside him. "Let's do this."

I grab my board and maneuver it so it's tucked under my arm. We make it across the street and to the sand, and I really hope no one is watching me. The board is really awkward and after a few minutes, my arms start to tire. It's not super heavy, just weird to carry.

"I really need to beef up these wimpy arms." I drop my board into the sand. "I didn't even make it halfway without dragging it."

Carson glances at me, surprised. "Your arms don't look that wimpy."

"Trust me. They are." I rub at my aching biceps while he puts the towels down.

He shuffles his feet and rubs the back of his neck. "Okay. So, the first thing you need to know about surfing? You're gonna fall. A lot."

"Great. That makes me want to jump in the waves right now."

He laughs. "No, really. Don't get discouraged. It takes a while to get used to balancing and knowing which wave to stand up on. You'll learn though."

I snort. Which makes us both laugh. Me more out of embarrassment. "We'll see about that." My balance sucks. Which I'm sure he'll figure out very soon.

"Oh, and you can swim, right? I forgot to ask."

I nod. "I swam in high school."

"Like on the swim team?"

"Yes. I know, I was a nerd."

"That's not nerdy at all. I'm just surprised. I thought you were more of a cheerleading or dancing type."

Oof, seriously?

"Um . . . that would be a no. I don't dance. I did take ballet when I was a kid, but it only lasted for about two months. My mom was pretty sad that I quit. She was on her high school drill team and everything so she wanted me to follow in her footsteps. It just wasn't for me."

"Those drill team girls are crazy dedicated. I wouldn't have lasted a day with all the stuff they have to do."

I chuckle. "I'm sure you would have been a great dancer."

He smiles as his cheeks redden. "Yeah . . . there's no way I'd be able to squeeze into those outfits, though."

"Probably a good thing." I bump his shoulder.

He bumps me back. "I know." He stops and rubs his hands together. "Well, are you ready to try your hand at surfing then? Hopefully you don't quit after our first lesson. I promise it's fun after you get used to it."

"Yep, I'm ready."

"Great." He gestures to my board lying in the sand. "Why don't you go ahead and hop on your board then."

I do as he says and step onto it.

"Now, lie down flat on it. You want that blue line to go right down the center of your body."

I move so I'm lying flat on my board. Hopefully he's not staring at my butt. I'm sure it looks really awesome right now. I move my arms so they're on either side of my face.

"Perfect. Now, when you're swimming out there, you want your toes to always be touching the back of the board. You use your arms to paddle. Not your feet." He moves so he's kneeling next to me. "Now. When a wave comes, I want you to pop up. And you have to do this part fast, but not so fast that you fall off. Put your arms right next to your chest and push yourself up so your arms are straight. Then lean back so you're kneeling, but you're sitting on your heels." He smiles as I do what he says. "Now, this is where it gets tricky. Put your right leg forward and leave your left leg back to balance. Once you get your balance, stand up."

I stand and laugh. I probably look ridiculous.

"What's so funny?"

"I'm a dork."

He smiles and shakes his head. "Now, once you're up on both feet, make sure the arches of your feet go through the middle of the line. If you're right in the middle of your board, you won't fall off as easy. Now, bend your knees and lean back," he says. I wobble, even though I'm on flat ground. He puts his hand on the small of my back to steady me. He leans in close and I can smell a hint of suntan lotion on him. "Put your arms straight out, like you see all the surfers do." I gulp and put my arms up. "If you lean forward, you'll wipe out. It's a fine line between leaning back too far, or leaning forward too far. You just have to find your own balance. Whatever feels comfortable to you." His breath tickles my ear and my heart beats like crazy.

"That doesn't sound too hard," I say. My voice is shaky. I want to tell the stupid butterflies in my stomach to go away. I shouldn't be feeling this way. Carson's just a friend, or rather, my surfing instructor. Nothing more. I don't have time for stupid crushes when I'm just going to leave in a few months.

"You okay?" Carson's watching me, a strange look on his face. I nod and fold my arms. "Um . . . why don't you get your wet suit on, and we'll go out and try some waves." He holds up a rope with what looks like a Velcro strap attached to the end of it. "I'll hook your leash to your board while you get ready."

"Leash?"

"It velcros around your ankle so you don't lose your board when you wipe out."

"Oh." I stand there, watching him loop it through a little hole on the back of my board I didn't even notice before.

He glances over and smiles at me. "You might want to get in that wet suit. It's pretty chilly out there."

"Okay." I try to ignore the fact that he's still staring at me and pick up the wet suit. It looks like it's made for a tiny little kid. Not someone curvy like me. How am I going to squeeze into something so small? Especially with people watching?

I sigh and realize I have to do it. I'm going to have to wear it whether I like it or not, otherwise I'll freeze to death.

The material is cold and rubbery. I don't want to put it on in front of Carson. I'm not even sure why it's a big deal, either. It's not like I'm stripping down naked. I'm putting something on to cover up. But it's tight. And I don't want him to see me struggle to get all of me in there.

"If you'd like me to turn around, I will."

I glance up and see Carson smiling at me. I swear he can read minds. Really. It's starting to creep me out. "That would be nice. Thank you." I hate how I'm so shy; I wish I could be like other girls and sport a bikini without a thought.

It takes me a minute to figure out how to put the wet suit on, but I get it. I zip it up as much as I can but I have to ask Carson to do the rest. His fingers are warm against my skin as he zips it all the way up to my neck, giving me chills. He gives it a little pat and steps back. "Perfect," he says.

I don't dare look down. I don't want to see what I look like. I'm sure it's horrifying.

"Okay, let's get your leash on." He bends down and wraps the Velcro around my ankle. It's uncomfortable, but at least I know I won't lose my board. "You'll get used to it," he says as though reading my thoughts. Again. "The rope is long enough that it won't bother you while you're surfing. You'll barely even notice it. Now, grab your board and let's go."

"Aren't you bringing yours?" I ask.

He shakes his head. "My foot's still bugging me. And all I'm going to do is help you today."

"But you won't have anything to hold on to."

"I'll be holding on to you most of the time." A flush of pink touches his cheeks and he turns around and runs a hand through his hair. "Besides, we're not going out that far. We're gonna stick with some smaller waves."

That sounds good to me.

I'm shocked at how cold the water is on my feet. The ocean is so deceiving. It always looks so peaceful and warm. Especially in the movies. Kids playing in the water, models swimming and coming out of the water while looking fabulous and hot.

They're all liars. It's freezing cold, just like the first time I touched the water. But that was only with my feet. Now that there's more of me in it, it's like standing butt naked in the snow cold. Not that I have any experience doing that, but I'm sure someone has and that they'd be just as cold.

We shuffle through the water and we're about up to our waists when I start to feel nervous. I hesitate going any farther, and he notices.

"You okay starting from here?" he asks.

"Are the waves big enough?" Just as the words leave my mouth, a wave breaks about a foot from me. It pushes me toward the beach and I struggle to keep my arms moving and make myself go forward. Carson just laughs. He's standing about chest deep and looks totally relaxed.

"We're good right here." He rubs his hands together. "Okay. Before we start, there's something called surfing etiquette that I need to teach you. Number one. The surfer closest to the peak of the wave gets to go first. We don't have to worry about it out here really, since most of the surfers are farther out, but when you get good enough, you have to remember that. You can't just hop on any wave you want."

I'm lost. "Peak?"

He grins. "When the white water starts falling from the wave."

"Oh. Right." Like white mountain peaks. Makes sense.

"Second. When someone's riding a wave, you can't just drop in front of them and cut them off. It makes for really angry surfers."

Like I'd even try something like that. I won't be able to drop in on anything. "Okay."

"Third. When you're paddling out here and someone is riding a wave, wait for them to pass before you paddle out farther so they don't run you over."

"Got it."

"Hang onto your board. If there's a huge wave while you're paddling out that you want to avoid, don't throw your board to avoid it."

"Why would I throw my board?"

He stares at me for a second before grinning. "Some people do because they panic. I can teach you the rest later. Now turn around and let's get started."

I'm nervous, but manage to turn myself around and feel Carson grab my board. "I'm gonna push you the first few times until you're used to it."

"Okay," I say.

"Here comes a good one. Get ready."

I'm ready. At least I tell myself I am. I brace myself, memorizing the blue line in the middle of my board.

My feet are supposed to go there. Right? Don't stand up too fast. Don't lean back too far. Everything jumbles together as I feel the wave push me forward. Before I can even think of getting to my feet, I fly off the side of my board.

A blast of cold hits me in the face and I get a mouthful of salt water. I struggle to the surface and feel my feet touch the bottom. I'm standing now, but coughing up water and cursing myself for thinking I could do it the first time.

My board is floating next to me, still attached to my ankle, as Carson wades over and puts a hand on my shoulder. "You okay?"

"Yes. Wasn't expecting the wave to go so fast."

He chuckles and grabs onto my arm to lift me up and over the water as another wave passes by. "Climb back on. Let's try it again."

I wipe the water from my face and get back on. I'm lying flat again and, as soon as I see the next wave coming, Carson shoves my board ahead of it. I push my upper body up, put my right foot forward, and crash headfirst into the water. The wave slams me to the bottom but I manage to figure out which way is up and pop my head out of the water a few seconds later. My eyes burn, but at least I kept my mouth closed this time.

I glance at Carson, who's wading toward me. He's so patient. If I were the teacher, I'd probably tell my student to find a new hobby.

We spend hours in the water. My fingers look like raisins and my arms and legs protest every time I move.

I'm about done but don't want to admit it. If I can get up once, just once, I'll feel like I accomplished something today. I can prove to myself that I can learn something new. I can make Lucas proud.

Carson is as patient as ever. He's encouraging and doesn't look bored at all. I'm sure he is, though. He's been watching me wipe out all morning. I paddle back to where he's standing and we wait for another wave. If I don't get up this time, I'm done.

I wait for it, see the peak, and push myself to my feet as it comes down. It all happens so fast. One second, I'm shaky and wobbly, and the next second, my arms are out and I'm steady as can be. I'm surfing. Actually surfing! I stand up straight, turn back to look at Carson, and he's clapping and shouting something. I let out a whoop and pump my fists in the air.

That's when I lose my balance and fall. Of course.

The wave brought me almost all the way to the beach, so I jump to my feet and wave Carson in. I'm exhausted, but so excited. I actually got up on a wave. Even if it was only for a second, it was so worth it.

My body is too tired to do anything else, so I unhook my surfboard leash and push my board onto the dry sand.

Once Carson's close enough, he runs over and wraps his arms around my waist. He swings me around and I laugh. "You did it!" he yells.

"I know! It was so awesome!" He sets me back on the ground. "Did you see me fall? I'm surprised I didn't swallow a bunch of water again. I closed my mouth just in time."

"Swallowing salt water's the worst. Trust me, I've been there."

"It's disgusting."

He chuckles and takes a step closer, his hand still on my waist. He searches my face for a moment and gives me a shy smile.

I tuck my wet hair behind my ear. "Thank you . . . for not laughing at me all day."

He steps back and folds his arms. "I've seen worse surfers than you, I promise."

"Probably little kids, right?"

He grins. "Maybe." We walk over to our towels to dry off. I sit down and set my board next to me. The sun feels good on my skin. Well, my face I guess, since everything else is covered by a wet suit.

He crouches down and runs his fingers across the middle of my board. "We need to get you some Sex Wax."

I blink. "Excuse me?"

He raises an eyebrow before chuckling. "It's wax for surfboards. You put it on the deck or the top of the surfboard so your feet get a little more traction. I put some on your board this morning, but we should probably get you your own since you're gonna be out here a bunch. We have all sorts of flavors at the shop. You can swing by and pick a few out."

"Okay. So . . . why do they call it Sex Wax? That's . . . interesting?"

He shrugs. "Just a brand name."

"Oh."

Carson looks at a watch on his wrist and curses. "I've gotta get to work." He unzips the top of his wet suit and rolls it down around his waist. I'm trying hard not to stare, like last time, but it's hard. He looks good. *Really* good. "What are you doing later?"

I pretend to be interested in the sand on my feet and shrug. "Not sure. Probably sleeping. I'm so tired."

"I'm sure you are. You did great, by the way."

"I need a lot of practice."

"Everyone does. You'll get it. I bet by the time the summer rolls around, you'll be a natural."

"Isn't a natural someone who actually does it perfect the first time?"

"Eh. Doesn't happen. Besides me."

I laugh and bury my feet deeper in the sand.

He glances at his watch again. "I've gotta go. My dad will kill me if I'm late." He stands and grabs his board, which is still in the same spot he left it. I'm surprised no one stole it. He's either really trustworthy or a lot of people know him and leave his stuff alone.

"Thanks for the lesson," I say.

"Anytime. Let me know when my first guitar lesson is." He smiles and heads toward his house.

My body hurts. I really don't want to walk back to Jo's house. Maybe I'll just take a nap on the beach instead.

Then I remember what I'm wearing. People will probably mistake me for a dead sea lion or something.

I pick up my board and towel and head back home.

When I open the front door, a voice greets me. "Did you have fun?"

I glance at Mom sitting at the counter. Her hands are wrapped around a coffee mug and she looks tired. "Yes. I got up on a wave, so I sort of know how to surf now."

"Good. I'm glad you had a good time."

I hesitate, but ask anyway. "Are you okay, Mom?"

She smiles. "I'm fine, honey. Just tired."

"You sure?"

She nods.

"Where were you yesterday? Jo said you went out but she didn't know where you went. I was . . . worried about you." It's hard to admit that last part, but it's true. I am worried about her.

"I just had to clear my head. I'm fine."

"Oh." I want her to say more. Explain to me why she had to clear her head. Because of Lucas? Dad? We stare at each other a moment before I clear my throat. "Um . . . I guess I'm gonna go change." She's acting weird. She never just sits around the house doing nothing. I know she hasn't showered and she's still in her robe from this morning.

"Oakley," she says.

"Mom?"

She searches my face for a moment before looking back at the mug in her hands. "Never mind."

Confused, I leave her alone. I'm not sure what to say to her anyway.

CHAPTER 9

DEAR OAKLEY,

HAVE I EVER TOLD YOU THAT HOSPITAL FOOD TASTES LIKE CRAP? NOT THAT I'VE ACTUALLY TASTED CRAP, BUT IF I HAD A CHOICE TO EAT EITHER, I'M SURE IT WOULD TASTE THE SAME. I'M SO READY FOR SOME HOMEMADE TURKEY NOODLE SOUP. OR MOM'S LASAGNA. YUM.

REMEMBER HOW MOM WOULD CUT OUR SANDWICHES IN TRIANGLES WHEN WE WERE LITTLE? OUR FRIENDS THOUGHT SHE WAS THE COOLEST MOM EVER. AND SHE WAS. MY FRIENDS LOVED COMING OVER TO HANG OUT BECAUSE SHE'D ALWAYS MAKE US SOME KIND OF TREAT.

IT'S KIND OF SAD. SHE'S CHANGED A LOT. IT'S MY FAULT. IF I WOULDN'T HAVE GOTTEN SICK, SHE'D BE THE SAME AS SHE USED TO BE. HAPPY. SHE DOESN'T SMILE MUCH ANYMORE. I KNOW IT'S BECAUSE OF ME. I DIDN'T MEAN TO MAKE EVERYONE SAD.

WHEN I'M GONE, TRY TO MAKE HER SMILE AGAIN. DAD, TOO. I'M SORRY THEY HAVEN'T BEEN THERE FOR YOU. I'M NOT MEANING TO TAKE ALL THE ATTENTION.

PLEASE DON'T BLAME THEM FOR IT OR BE TOO HARD ON THEM. THEY'VE BEEN THROUGH A LOT, TOO.

ANYWAY. EAT SOME LASAGNA FOR ME. AND SCONES. SCONES AND HONEY BUTTER ARE MY FAVORITE. BUT OF COURSE YOU KNOW THAT.

LOVE, LUCAS

I let out the breath I'm holding as I set the notebook down and sit on the edge of my bed. I stare at the floor. Don't be too hard on Mom and Dad, he says. It's hard not to be. I understand they've gone through a lot but at least they have each other. Or *had* each other. Lucas was the one person I had and now I have no one.

The nights Mom and Dad fought come back full force. Lucas taking me outside when we were ten and twelve, trying to shelter me from the reality of our lives. My parents didn't always fight. When we were younger, they were happy. We were all rather close. But as we got older, Mom and Dad cared about their careers more than each other, it seemed, and it built a wedge between them. And us.

They weren't bad parents. I know they loved us. But we weren't "close" like some families I know. "Close," to them, was living in the same house together and talking for a bit each day, but not supporting us in our hobbies and things. Not really *knowing* us, I guess. But while my parents weren't there, Lucas always was. He helped me with my homework all through middle school, came to all of my swim meets when I was a sophomore and a junior. Made me dinner half the time, since I'm a terrible cook and Mom and Dad were always home too late. He was the one who comforted me when he got diagnosed and my parents freaked out and shut down. He was always there for me. It didn't matter what it was. He was always there.

Was.

I shake my head. I don't want to think about that right now. Instead, I lie back on my bed and look up at the ceiling.

My cell rings on the nightstand and I lean over to see who it is.

Dad. He hasn't talked to me since I got here. I'm sure he's been busy but he could have at least called to see how I was doing. Or I guess I could have called him too. I put the phone to my ear. "Hello?"

"Hey, pumpkin. How's it going?"

I smile at the word *pumpkin*. He's called me that since I was a little kid. "Hi, Dad. I'm good."

"You adjusting to Jo's house?"

"Yep. It's nice here." It takes me a minute to think of the right word. "Relaxing."

"Good. I just wanted to see how you're doing. I've talked to your mother a few times, but not you."

"Thanks. I was wondering when you'd call."

There's a moment's hesitation but he continues. "They put up Lucas's headstone today."

100

I can't say anything because of the sudden lump in my throat.

"It looks nice. There's a basketball on it and a car. He loved working on his car."

"I know. His stupid, crappy car. I don't know why he loved that thing so much." My lip trembles and I fight to keep myself together. I clear my throat and blink, forcing the moisture in my eyes away. "I'm glad it looks good. Can you text me a picture?"

"Sure." He's quiet. "I think about him every day. I visit his grave after work. There are still a lot of flowers there. It looks nice."

As nice as a grave could look. "Thank you for visiting him, Daddy." I sniff. "I miss you." It's true. Even though we have our days, Dad has always been around. It's weird not having him here with us.

"I miss you too."

"Are you gonna come visit?" I have a sinking feeling that he won't be coming any time soon. If at all. But I have to ask.

"I'm not sure. Your mother and I . . . I'll talk to her. I'd love to come see you. It just depends on work."

Of course it does. "Well, I hope you can come before the spring's over. I can teach you how to surf."

"Really?"

"No. But I sort of learned how to stay up for five seconds yesterday. It was fun."

"I'd love to see that."

I smile. He could see it if he'd stop being so stubborn and just hop on a plane.

"Well, I'll talk to you later. I have some things I need to take care of. I love you, pumpkin. Call me anytime you need me, okay?"

"Okay."

We say goodbye and I hang up the phone.

Normally, when I was feeling down, he'd give me a hug or pat me on the shoulder before leaving me. My stomach drops. I wonder if going from parent to parent and being in the middle of their fights will be a permanent thing. I hope they're working it out. I'm sure the stress of losing their only son has taken its toll on their marriage, but we're a family. Families are supposed to work things out.

The rest of the day is uneventful. After running to the store, getting a few pictures developed, and hanging them on my wall, I spend most of my time pacing the floor in my room, trying to figure out what to do with myself.

By the time ten o'clock rolls around, everyone's in bed. Jo was at work all day, Mom spent most of the day in her room again, and I haven't seen Carson since he went to work yesterday. I don't want to admit I miss hanging out with him. Especially since it's only been a day since I saw him. I don't want to feel like that. It seems needy. And I'm not a needy person.

I should probably change into my pajamas and go to sleep. Maybe I'll practice my surfing stance tomorrow morning on the beach. Or I could stand in the small waves and practice balancing. It's not like I have anything else to do.

A small tapping noise comes from my French doors. Curious, I walk over and peek through the curtain.

It's Carson. Holy crap—I look hideous.

I brush my hair out of my face, take a quick glance in the mirror next to me, decide nothing will help, and open the door. "Hey," I say.

"Hi."

"Sneaking into Jo's backyard now?"

He grimaces. "Sorry about that. I should get your number so I can text you."

"No worries. What's up?"

"I know it's late, but I saw your light on and wondered if you wanted to go for a walk with me." He swallows and his lips part slightly.

It *is* late. But it's also really tempting to leave. A hot guy sneaking out just to hang out with me? Like I'm not going to go. "Let me grab a jacket or something. You can come in."

He steps inside and looks around. His eyes go to the pictures on the wall above my headboard. "Wow. You really do take awesome pictures."

I shrug. "Not really."

He eyes me with a strange expression. "No. Really." He walks over to my bed and inspects them. "I recognize this guy," he says. His expression is strange. He's smiling but looks a little annoyed.

"Yes, that's Dillon. But I have a bunch of other surfers on there too." I'm not sure why I say that. I doubt he's jealous or anything but I find myself wanting to make sure he doesn't think my focus is ever on Dillon on purpose.

He laughs. "These are really good. You should sell some of them to a magazine or something."

I laugh and grab a hoodie out of the closet. "Trust me. No one would want those."

When I turn around, he's right in front of me. He stares down at me with a frown on his face. "You don't give yourself enough credit," he says. "Why can't you just say thank you when someone compliments you?"

I'm not sure what to say, but I do know I'm staring. His gaze is unflinching and serious but I can see a hint of a smile as well. "I—uh—thanks. I guess." I avoid his eyes and step around him. "You ready to go?"

"Do you have to let your mom know where we're going?"

"She doesn't care." I slide on my flip-flops and walk out the door. He follows me and shuts it softly behind him. It's dark but we head down to the beach anyway. There are some lights on the boardwalk, so we can at least see a little bit. I slip on my hoodie. It's not too cold but I feel more snug in it. "So, where're we going?" I ask.

He shrugs. "I just like the beach at night. It's not as . . . eventful as it is during the day. No people running around splashing in the water. It's nice. Relaxing."

"Makes sense."

We walk in comfortable silence as I kick the cold sand and smile. I haven't felt this calm for a while. I attempt to keep my worries and thoughts of Lucas away for a moment and just think of the beautiful place I'm living. Carson's right. It's much more relaxing at night.

We keep walking and I glance up. The lights on Huntington Pier grow bright as we get closer and I can hear the waves crashing into it as well. "This is such a pretty place," I say.

"It is. Why don't you tell me what *your* place is like?"

"Utah?"

He nods. "I've never been."

"It's not as cool as here. Lots of mountains, grass, a lot of snow in the winter."

"I may take you up on having your dad ship you some snow."

"Trust me. It's nice to look at but it gets old quick. And it's so cold. I'm not a fan of the cold."

"You chose the wrong place to live then." He chuckles.

"My parents chose the wrong place to live." I smile. "But it's home, I guess."

"Maybe I can convince you to stay here longer. Since you can't stand the cold and all."

"I do enjoy warm weather." I laugh. "I sound like I'm fifty."

"You don't look it." His fingers brush my hand and before I know it, they're entwined with mine. He looks over and gives me a small smile. "Is this okay?"

I smile a little too and nod. His hand warms mine and I can't help but notice how well they fit together. Which is stupid. I'm sure all hands fit together the same. I think back to the only guy I've ever held hands with. Back before Lucas got sick. It wasn't like this at all. He was kind of weird. And his hand was sweaty and gross. Obviously things didn't work out.

Carson points up ahead. "My sister and I used to play under the pier when we were little. Not at night since the tide is so high, but my mom would bring us down and we'd run around the posts and hide from each other. Or we'd try picking barnacles off them with sticks. That was always fun."

"Barnacles. Those weird little shell things, right?"

"Yeah. Have you never seen one?"

I shake my head. "Not in person, just in pictures."

"I'll show you sometime. They're pretty weird, but I was obsessed with them as a kid."

"Boys. Always obsessed with weird things."

He laughs and squeezes my hand. "So, what did you do in high school besides swimming? Anything interesting?"

"Not really. What about you?"

"Oh, come on. I'm sure there's something you did."

"Nothing worth mentioning. You already know I play guitar, swim, and take pictures. What about you?"

He shrugs. "I played a little football."

I knew it. I don't know how I did, but I knew it. "Cool."

He smiles. "Not a fan of football?"

"Not really."

"Makes sense. You still seem like a choir girl to me." He looks at me out of the corner of his eye and chuckles at my expression.

"I've already confessed that I can't sing."

"You can't be *that* bad."

"Really. I'm horrible."

He chuckles. "I'd still like to hear you, even though you think you suck."

"Not gonna happen," I say. "Really. It's pitiful. My brother is an awesome singer." I realize what I've said and sigh. Was. *Was* an awesome singer.

"My sister's like you say you are. She can't sing at all. It's hilarious." His eyes widen. "Not that it's funny that *you* can't sing, I just like making fun of *her*."

"Right," I say, letting the sarcasm drip. "Like I said. No singing in front of you. Ever."

"Ah, you're no fun." He nudges me with his shoulder.

I let go of his hand and stop to slip my flip-flops off and walk out near the water. I love feeling the wet sand between my toes. It's kind of like a pedicure. Carson does the same but leaves his flip-flops on.

"How's your foot?" I ask. I haven't seen him surfing yet but the bandage is gone.

He shrugs. "Better. I still have the cut covered, just a small bandage though. It itches."

"That means it's healing." At least that's what my dad always told me when I got hurt. "I think." I smile, knowing I have no idea what I'm talking about.

"Thank you, Dr. Nelson."

I chuckle. "I'm glad to be of service."

We walk in easy silence, enjoying each other's company. There are a lot of people out. A few walking dogs on the boardwalk. There are several couples holding hands, like us, and a few on the beach tucked under blankets doing who knows what. I see a few kids with their parents and wonder why they aren't in bed, but obviously it's none of my business. I smile at a family as they walk by us. Everyone I've seen so far has one thing in common: they look so happy. So at peace with the world.

I stare out into the dark, catching the glimmer of boat lights every now and then. That's what my life is like right now. Dark, but with a glimmer of hope on the horizon. I'm trying to move on. Trying to forget what I've been through, but I know it will take some time. At least I'm feeling a little normal again. Whatever normal is.

"Do you want to talk about it?"

I look over and Carson isn't looking at me but I know he's been watching me.

"Not really." I should. I really should talk about it. Maybe it would help, but it's too new. Too fresh on my mind. I can't do it. Not yet.

"Whatever it is that makes you sad, I'm sorry." He glances at me, a serious expression on his face. "You can talk to me, you know."

"I barely know you." It's true. We both know it. Yet I feel more comfortable with him than I ever have with anyone else. Which is strange. I'm not used to trusting so easily.

His eyes lighten and I catch a small smile. "Why don't we change that? What do you want to know?"

I think for a moment and stop walking. "Hmmm . . ." I start. "Let me think for a minute." I squish my toes in the sand. The water covers my feet and I shiver. I feel the pull of the ocean as the wave goes back in. It tries to pull me with it but I let my feet sink deeper. I look up to find Carson watching me. The corner of his mouth twitches but he says nothing. "What?" I ask.

"Are you having fun?"

"Yes." I realize I'm supposed to be thinking of a question. "So, you sort of own your own surf shop. Are you going to do that for a living?"

It's lame but the only thing I can think of. I'm surprised when he frowns.

"I don't know." He scratches his head and stares at the water.

Curious at his reaction, I keep going. "You don't know? Don't you like it there?"

He nods. "It's fine. I just don't want to be stuck there forever. I want to go to college."

I think back to one of the first conversations we ever had. "A marine veterinarian, right?"

"Right. It's just . . ." He hesitates and then sighs. "My dad wants me to take over permanently. Run the surf shop for him. It's a family thing and it does very well, but that's not what I want to do forever. It's his dream to see me take over and expand the store. To pass it down to my kids and keep it going. And I don't want to do it."

"Have you talked to him about it?" I don't know why I'm attempting to give advice. I can't even talk to my own parents.

He shrugs. "He doesn't really listen. Don't get me wrong, I love the guy, but . . . I just have different goals than he does."

I put a hand on his arm and the motion shocks even me, but I leave it there. "You should talk to him again. You could work through college running the shop but then he has to understand you have your own dreams."

"That's the problem. He never went to college and thinks it's a waste of money." He lets out an annoyed laugh. "Unless I go into business because that will help the shop. He just doesn't understand why I'd go to school for anything else since I'm basically being handed a full-time job for the rest of my life." He lets out a frustrated sigh. "Can we talk about something else?"

I'm still curious but nod anyway. I look down at my feet and try to move. I've sunk well past my ankles and if I pull one foot out, I'll probably fall over. That would be super awesome. "Um . . . a little help?"

He laughs and grabs my hand, pulling me out. I somehow trip over my own feet and crash into his chest. He grabs me around the waist to steady himself but we both fall over anyway.

The side of my face slams into the cold sand. I let out a surprised scream as a little wave comes in and I feel cold water seeping through my jeans. Carson is laughing his head off next to me as I stand up.

I glance at my butt, noting the wetness. Nice. "Great. It looks like I peed my pants."

"Me too," he says with a laugh,

I can taste grains of sand in my mouth so I rub my lips with my hand to try and get the saltiness off.

"That didn't quite go as planned," he says, brushing sand out of his hair.

"No kidding." I spit sand out of my mouth as I think of how many people probably walked on it that day.

Disgusting.

"That was attractive."

I glare at him. "What was I supposed to do? It was in my mouth!" I walk over to dry sand and sit down, knowing full well it'll be stuck to my wet pants the rest of the night. Oh well.

He laughs again as he takes a seat next to me and we ease into comfortable silence.

The stars are beautiful tonight. I don't remember the stars being so bright in Utah. Maybe I just didn't pay attention. I never had time to pay attention.

Carson's leg brushes mine and I realize how close we're sitting. I study him as he looks down the beach. Before I let myself get too comfortable, I wipe my sandy hands off and stand. "I should probably be getting back."

He looks disappointed and opens his mouth to say something but shuts it. He stands, hesitates a second, and takes the hand I offer him. "You're right."

Even though I say I need to get back, we take our time. Twenty minutes later, we make our way through the back fence of Jo's house. Carson walks me to my bedroom door and I silently start freaking out. It's the doorstep scene all over again. I gulp and take a deep breath before I turn to face him. "Thanks for the walk. I needed it tonight."

He shrugs. "Anytime." He searches my face and clears his throat. "I'll . . . uh . . . see you tomorrow then."

"Okay." I pull my hand away. It tingles from his touch and I'm surprised how much I want him to stay.

"Goodnight, Oakley." He gives me a shy smile, walks to the fence, and lets himself out. I stare at the fence until I hear his door close.

I don't want to admit it but I may have a crush. Just a little one.

CHAPTER 10

DEAR OAKLEY,

YOU KNOW THAT SUPER MARIO BLANKET MOM BOUGHT ME FOR MY BIRTHDAY WHEN I WAS FIVE? I STILL HAVE IT. I TOLD MOM I GOT RID OF IT A FEW YEARS AGO BECAUSE I THOUGHT I WAS TOO OLD FOR MARIO. BUT THE TRUTH IS, MARIO ROCKS. I MEAN, HOW COOL WOULD IT BE TO BE A PLUMBER GUY WHO'S REALLY SHORT AND FAT BUT CAN STILL JUMP REALLY HIGH? THAT'S AWESOME! AND ON TOP OF THAT, HE GETS PRINCESS PEACH FOR A GIRLFRIEND. EVEN WITH HER ANNOYING SAYINGS ON MARIO KART. EVEN THOUGH DAISY IS CUTER. ALTHOUGH, I DO PREFER BRUNETTES, SO THAT'S PROBABLY WHY. STUPID LUIGI. I NEVER LIKED HIM AND HIS CREEPY VOICE.

ANYWAY, I'M NOT REALLY SURE WHAT THIS LETTER HAS TO DO WITH ANYTHING TODAY. I WAS JUST THINKING ABOUT THAT BLANKET. IT'S SHOVED IN THE TOP OF MY CLOSET. YOU CAN SNUGGLE WITH IT IF YOU WANT. JUST REMEMBER IT WAS ON MY BED FOR YEARS. AND I TOOK IT EVERYWHERE. IT'S PROBABLY REALLY DISGUSTING NOW, SO IT WOULD BE A GOOD IDEA TO WASH IT BEFORE YOU SLEEP

WITH IT. BECAUSE YOU WILL SLEEP WITH IT. IT'S MARIO. WHO WOULDN'T WANT SOME OF THAT ACTION?

SWEET DREAMS!

LOVE, LUCAS

I stare at the letter. He *still* has that nasty old blanket? I remember it well. He took it everywhere with him. Sometimes Mom had to drag it out of his hands. She always said he was too old to carry a blanket around, even though she was the one who gave it to him. And it wasn't like he took it into the grocery store or anything. Though I wouldn't put it past him.

So many memories.

Someone taps on my door and Mom walks in before I answer. "Hey," she says. She looks a little better today. Her hair is done and she's wearing makeup. She sits down on the edge of my bed and pulls on a piece of her hair. She always does that when she's nervous. "There's something I need to talk to you about."

Here it comes. I already know what it is. I've seen the signs. Ever since Lucas got diagnosed with cancer, she and Dad have acted differently toward one another. I don't think they blame each other, since you can't give cancer to anyone, but I think they both wish they could have done more. "It's about you and Dad. I talked to him last night."

She looks at me, surprised. "You did?"

114

"He didn't say anything about you but I'm not stupid, Mom. I figured it out before we even got here."

"Oakley." She sighs. "Your father and I . . ." She frowns and I know she's unsure of what to say or how to say it.

"You're getting divorced." I look away from her penetrating gaze and focus on my hands. Anything to distract myself from looking at her. "There. I said it for you so you didn't have to do it."

"Oakley . . . let me explain. It's not like—"

"It's fine, Mom. I knew it was coming." I fling my covers off my legs and slip my flip-flops on. "I'll be on the beach if you need me."

"Oakley, wait. It's not fine. We need to talk about this."

"I don't want to. I know what a divorce means."

She lets out a frustrated breath. "That's not what I meant."

I put my hand on the doorknob. "Then what do you mean?"

"We just need to talk. I need you to understand what I'm going through."

I frown. "What *you're* going through? Have you ever thought about what *I'm* going through? I'm seventeen and I've been through way more than most people my age have. And that's not a good thing. My parents forgot about me for the past year and are now getting divorced. My brother was diagnosed with cancer, and I watched him die. I. Watched. Him. *Die.* My best friend is gone. And my

115

mom can't even look me in the eye and tell me it's going to be okay."

Her eyes fill with tears and I take a shaky breath to keep mine at bay. "Oakley—"

I hold up a hand to stop her. "Please." *Keep breathing.* "I can't do this right now." Even though I *want* to say more. I want her to know how much I'm hurting. I want her to know how much their divorce is already affecting me, how it's their fault I'm the way I am, but I can't bring myself to do it. So I stand there and stare at her, my hand still on the doorknob, her sad eyes still on me. Begging me for . . . I'm not sure what. I think back to Lucas's letter from yesterday. *Don't be too hard on Mom and Dad.* How can I not be? Can't she see how much I'm hurting? How much pain I'm in from losing the three people I care about most? Before I say something I regret, I turn away. "I'll be back later," I say and open the door.

"Oakley, please."

I shut the door and leave her alone.

I'm fuming by the time I reach the water. I don't know whether to cry or to punch something. Or someone. My family has completely fallen to crap. It's killing me to watch their marriage fall apart by myself.

It sucks. A lot.

Lucas would have handled this so much better than me. He looked on the bright side of everything, even when there wasn't one. If he were here, he'd put a positive spin on things. If he were here, he'd tell me to quit acting

116

like a baby and man up. The corner of my mouth twitches, thinking of all the times he said that to me because he knew how much I hated it.

But now I realize how true the statement is. I *am* acting like a baby. Lucas may be gone but my parents are still here. And all I'm doing is pushing them away.

I debate going to see what Carson's doing, since he always seems to put me in a better mood but decide against it. His Jeep is gone so I'm sure he's at work. And I'm not really brave enough to show up and meet his family without him there.

"Hey, Oakley."

I turn around and see Dillon striding toward me with a smile on his face. I know he lives around here but not sure where. "Hi," I say. I'm distracted. I don't really want to talk to anyone. I hate fighting with Mom. Hate it.

"You busy?"

I shake my head. "Not really."

"Why don't I take you to breakfast? Have you eaten?"

"No." I force a smile but my mind keeps racing. Maybe I was too hard on Mom. I should apologize but I don't know what I'd say. "I'm not very hungry though."

He looks disappointed.

"Sorry. Maybe another time."

"I'll hold you to that."

We stand in awkward silence until he clears his throat beside me. "You want to go for a walk or something? I don't have to work for another hour."

I shrug. "Okay."

We walk. My mind is scattered so I don't talk. Just listen. It's not like Dillon asks me any questions anyway. He has no problem carrying on the conversation himself. He talks and talks and I sort of tune him out for a while.

"Have you tried it yet?"

I look over at him, still distracted. "Huh?"

He smiles. "Surfing."

"Oh. Yes. Carson took me out yesterday."

His smile falters but he recovers quickly. "He wasn't working yesterday . . . he must have given you a freebie."

"A freebie?"

"He taught you for free. That's not normal for him. He usually doesn't do that for his students."

"I'm not really his student. We're just friends."

He chuckles. "Sure."

I stop walking. "No, really. He's become a good friend."

He holds his hands out defensively. "I wasn't implying anything. I'm just curious. I've known Carson for years and he never just gives someone surf lessons. Or hangs out with them all the time. He's pretty private. He's had girls after him for years and hasn't given them a second glance. But then you come along and he's hooked."

"It's not like that."

He smiles. "Maybe not for you. I can tell you've got him wrapped around your finger though."

I fold my arms and start walking again. "You've never even seen us together." Why is he telling me this anyway? It's hard to believe Carson may like me that much already.

118

He doesn't know anything about me. Other than I can't surf and I can't sing.

"I've seen enough."

I stop again and he does as well. "I should probably be getting back" I say.

"Really?"

"Yes. I have some things I need to do today."

He studies me and I shrink under his gaze. "Do you want me to walk you back?"

I shake my head. "I can manage. Thanks for the walk."

"Anytime. And I'm really taking a rain check on that breakfast."

"Okay." I start back home, very aware of his eyes on me. I'm not sure why I'm annoyed but I am. And confused.

The rest of the day consists of the silent treatment from Mom. And no word from Carson.

CHAPTER 11

DEAR OAKLEY,

IT'S TIME WE HAD A TALK. AND NO, NOT ABOUT THE BIRDS AND THE BEES. THAT WOULDN'T BE AWKWARD AT ALL . . .

I chuckle. Even when he was in the hospital, he still had a sense of humor. I could just hear his sarcasm.

BUT SERIOUSLY. I KNOW HOW GUYS THINK. BE CAREFUL. YOU'RE GETTING CUTE. THAT'S THE WORD I'LL USE, SINCE YOU'RE MY LITTLE SISTER. PICK A GUY WHO WILL TREAT YOU WITH RESPECT. SOMEONE LIKE ME, BUT NOT ME. FUNNY, BRILLIANT, AND ALL OUT AWESOME. AND IF YOU FIND THE RIGHT GUY, DON'T SCREW IT UP BY BEING SOMEONE YOU'RE NOT. BE YOURSELF. GUYS DON'T LIKE FAKE GIRLS. AND YOU'RE NOT FAKE.

OH, AND STAY AWAY FROM BRADY COLIER. SERIOUSLY. IF HE EVEN TRIES TO HIT ON YOU, YOU HAVE MY PERMISSION TO KICK HIM IN THE NUTS.

LOVE, LUCAS

Brady Colier. I'll admit he's hot but that's about it. Lucas has nothing to worry about as far as Brady's concerned.

I set Lucas's notebook down and pull on some shorts and a tank top. The news about my parents getting divorced simmers at the back of my mind. I try not to think about it. Try not to worry. I'll deal with it when I'm ready.

A part of me knows I should talk to Mom. Fix what's already broken between us, but I can't. I don't know how to fix it. I don't know what to say.

My cell rings and I flop down on my bed and pick it up.

"Hello?"

"Hey, Oakley. Sorry I didn't call yesterday. My dad had me work a twelve-hour shift. I was beat when I got home so I went straight to bed."

"Sounds rough."

"Eh. It wasn't a big deal."

"Good."

"So, do you want to catch some waves later today? I'm heading to work right now but I'll meet you on the beach around three if you want. We can try some bigger waves today."

"That would be great."

"Also, my family wants to meet you. My sister, anyway. Do you want to come over for dinner?"

My heart quickens. He wants me to meet his *family*? Maybe that whole conversation with Dillon yesterday was true. Did he really like me like *that*? "Uh . . . sure."

"Great! I'll see you later then."

"Okay. Bye."

I hang up the phone. Maybe hanging out with Carson will distract me from the mess that has become my life. I don't know how I feel about meeting his family but I decide to take it one step at a time. Breathe in and breathe out. Worry about it later.

I will worry about it *all* later.

Instead of sulking in my room until three, I grab my surfboard and head to the beach. A little practice will do me good before I make a fool out of myself in front of Carson again.

It's kind of stormy but there are a few people surfing anyway. The water's choppy, so I stay near the beach to practice on smaller waves coming in. I'm surprised how easy it's getting for me to stand. My legs are still sore from the day Carson taught me but I can feel them getting used to the movement of jumping up and balancing. The leash around my ankle doesn't bother me at all anymore.

I know I've been out for a few hours but I need as much practice as I can get.

After riding another small wave in, I jump off my board. The water laps at my feet as I stare out into the ocean at the surfers riding the bigger waves. Something sparks inside me. Maybe I could try the big waves without Carson. It doesn't look too different from what I've already been doing.

I shake my head. I'm never spontaneous. I don't do things that could be dangerous. But . . . why not? Would it be so bad to break my good girl habit once in a while and do something impulsive? What would it hurt to go out and try the big waves? It's not like I'll drown or anything. I'm a good swimmer. And even if I did drown, it wouldn't be the end of the world.

I hang my head and rub my eyes. Why would that thought even enter my mind? I don't want to die. Do I?

I stare out at the waves. There are pros and cons to the idea, for sure. Like seeing Lucas again. I could be happy. Just me and him. No one would even realize I was gone. My friends have already forgotten about me. I'm sure Mom and Dad would be sad but Mom thinks I'm suicidal anyway. She wouldn't be too surprised. I wonder if she'd miss me.

Before I know what's happening, I'm paddling out past the smaller waves. I kick and dig my arms into the water, fighting the current pushing me back toward shore, and finally make it to where the other surfers are. I watch them wait their turns to take different waves, one after the other. They're all so calm. Like they've been surfing for years. None of them look as nervous as I feel. No one even looks at me, so I hang back and watch, trying to figure out the right technique to it all.

My body is shaking but it might be because of the cold. Or maybe adrenaline has taken over. I wait until the last one catches a wave and moves out of sight.

Now what am I supposed to do?

The cold seeps through my wet suit and caresses my skin. I shiver. The water's dark and murky and the waves

look extra big. Dangerous. I'm doing something dangerous. Which makes me smile. I think of Lucas then, knowing exactly what he'd say if he were with me.

Don't be stupid, Oakley.

I'm not being stupid. I'm trying something new and
taking risks.

I look around. There's no one near me. No one to give
me pointers or tell me I'm going to be okay. For some reason, it makes me more determined. I *can* take risks. I *can* do
hard things. And I *am* going to get up on a wave and ride
it back to the beach.

After closing my eyes for a moment, I take a deep
breath and start kicking. A swell is coming toward me and
I paddle along and watch the wave break. I feel it push my
board. Hard. I slide my foot forward and crouch, just like
I did on the smaller waves, but lean forward too far. My
arms flail and I fall.

My eyes are open when I hit the water. They burn and
sting at the same time. The wave rolls me around and I
have no idea which way is up. I try to swim and even open
my eyes again but all I can see is darkness. I'm surrounded
by darkness. And cold.

My hands touch the bottom and I move my body so
my feet push off the sand and launch me toward the top.
My breath is almost gone when I finally reach the surface
and I gasp as my head comes out of the water.

I try to wipe the salt out of my eyes and a wave pushes
me under again. I swallow a mouthful as I get hit by
another one. They keep coming and coming, pushing me

down every single time. I have no idea where my board is. I struggle to stay afloat and try to swim but I'm so disoriented I'm not sure where to go. Maybe I really will die . . .

And now I'm not sure I'm okay with that.

I break the surface once more and someone shouts next to me. The voice sounds far away but familiar. I'm surprised when a hand grabs my arm and pulls me up.

"Oakley! I'm right here." I blink the salt water out of my eyes and focus on Carson's face. His dark eyes are filled with worry. "Can you swim?"

I nod and attempt to put one arm in front of the other.

"I've got you." He wraps an arm around me and pulls me along with him until I can touch the ground. I lean against him as he helps me out of the water. We make it to the beach and I fall to my knees in the sand. I've swallowed a bunch of salt water and cough half of it up.

"Are you okay?"

I swipe my sticky wet hair out of my eyes and take a shaky breath. "I'm fine." I should have listened to Lucas. *Don't be stupid.* Because that's exactly what I was. Stupid. "Where's my board?" I know it's not hooked to my ankle anymore since I felt it rip away when the wave took me down.

"I'm not worried about your board, I'm worried about you." He crouches down to my level but I don't look at him. "You're sure you're okay?"

I nod and glance up. He looks relieved and then his expression changes; he doesn't look concerned at all anymore. The muscles in his jaw are clenched and his face is flushed. He looks furious. He grabs my hands and tries to pull me to my feet but I'm too wobbly and fall back in the sand. I let go of his hands and wrap my arms around my middle, taking big shaky breaths. He doesn't say anything, just waits until I'm ready. Once I've calmed down a bit, I reach out a hand and he helps me up. My legs wobble again but I think I'm okay.

"Sorry. My legs aren't cooperating."

He watches me for a second, a concerned look on his face, and then . . . he loses it. "Would you like to explain to me what exactly you were thinking out there?"

"Excuse me?"

"Were you trying to kill yourself? Because you were doing a pretty good job."

I frown. "No, I wasn't trying to kill myself. I was trying to surf!"

He takes a step closer, his arms folded. "I told you to wait for me. We were going to go out there together so I could teach you. But by the looks of those waves? Not a good day for a newbie to surf. They're too choppy and dangerous. *I* wouldn't even go out there on a day like this."

"Well, I'm sorry I didn't get the memo."

He frowns. "You're not funny."

"I'm not trying to be."

He stares at me for a second and shakes his head. "I don't get you. Your moods are so unpredictable. One second you'll be smiling and laughing and the next you have some far-off look in your eyes and a frown on your face.

126

Whatever is making you look like that—it's not worth killing yourself over."

My temper flares. "You have no idea what you're talking about. And I wasn't trying to kill myself!"

"You could have fooled me."

"I was struggling and trying to get out of the water!"

"You weren't trying very hard. For being on the swim team in high school, you should have been able to get back to the beach with no problem. I know you're a stronger swimmer than that." The look he gives me is pained. "I saw you stop swimming, Oakley. You gave up."

"I didn't give up."

He ignores me. "You're lucky I came when I did. No one else even saw you."

"How did *you* see me then?"

"I saw you fall off your board so I knew where you went under."

I don't know what to say so I stare at the sand between my toes.

He's quiet for a moment and then he speaks again. Quiet and controlled. "Tell me you didn't try to drown yourself."

"I didn't." I look up, surprised at the expression on his face. He looks sad. Which confirms he doesn't believe me. And then I surprise even myself by adding, "And even if I did, it wouldn't be so bad? . . . I have nothing to lose."

"You have everything to lose."

"No. I don't. My brother's already gone. I have nothing."

He stares at me. Curious. "Your parents."

"Don't talk to me about my parents. You don't know them. Or me."

He reaches out and runs his fingers across my cheek. "I can help you. Talk to me and let me help."

"I don't think anyone can help me right now." I step away from his touch and turn around.

"Oakley," he says, his calm voice sends a mixture of emotions rushing through me but I don't look back as I make my way back to the house, and he doesn't follow.

So much for being spontaneous. This is *so* like me.

CHAPTER 12

I escape to the only place I can think of: my room. I change out of my stupid wet suit but don't bother putting my wet hair in a ponytail. I feel gross from the salty water but I'm too exhausted and upset to get in the shower.

Lucas's notebook is sitting on the bed where I left it earlier. I need to read his words. They'll comfort me. He always knows what to say. He'll make this all go away. I sniff, take a deep breath, and read.

DEAR OAKLEY,

IT'S BEEN A HARD DAY. NOT GONNA LIE. I'M USUALLY PRETTY UPBEAT, BUT FOR SOME REASON, TODAY IS A DOWN DAY. YOU KNEW SOMETHING WAS WRONG WHEN YOU CAME TO VISIT ME EARLIER, BUT YOU KNOW HOW I AM. I PRETEND I'M FINE, EVEN IF YOU KNOW I'M NOT. I CAN'T HELP BUT THINK SOMETIMES, WHY DID THIS HAPPEN TO ME? WHY WAS I THE ONE TO GET SICK? I KNOW EVERYTHING HAPPENS FOR A REASON, BUT IT'S HARD TO THINK OF WHAT THAT REASON IS.

I KNOW I'M GOING TO BE OKAY. I'M NOT AFRAID OF DYING. IN FACT, I'M EXCITED FOR A NEW ADVENTURE. ONE THAT WON'T INVOLVE NEEDLES OR CHEMICALS,

PAIN AND WEAKNESS. I'LL BE WHOLE AGAIN. MYSELF. IT'S KIND OF CYNICAL TO WANT TO DIE, BUT I DON'T HAVE ANYTHING LEFT TO DO HERE. BESIDES SUFFER. AND OF COURSE, BEAT YOU AT X-BOX.

THE ONLY THING IN THIS WORLD I'LL MISS IS YOU. MOM AND DAD A LITTLE, BUT MOSTLY YOU. YOU'RE MY BABY SISTER. MY BEST FRIEND. PLEASE TAKE CARE OF YOURSELF AND MOVE ON WHEN I'M GONE. DON'T STAY IN THE PAST, BUT DON'T FORGET ME. PROMISE ME YOU WON'T FORGET ME.

LOVE, LUCAS

Tears stream down my cheeks as a familiar image flashes through my mind of Lucas hooked up to all those machines. His thin face smiling all the time, even when he was too sick to speak. He was braver than I'll ever be. And I miss him so much it hurts.

His words ring inside my mind. He didn't want to die but was okay with it. I shiver. I could have died today. And no matter what I may think and say, I know I'm not ready to die. Even if Lucas is gone, there's so much I haven't experienced yet. So many things I want to do. And how can I even think of throwing away my life when Lucas fought so hard to keep his?

Carson was right. What was I thinking?

A knock on my French doors makes me jump. I'm afraid to open it. I'm sure it's Carson. Why did he follow me? I wipe my eyes and go to the door. It takes me a minute before I've calmed down enough to open it.

Carson stands on my porch holding my surfboard. He doesn't smile, just searches my face. His eyes are sad and he's looking at me with such concern that my eyes fill again.

He leans the board against the side of the house and takes a step toward me. I want to run, to hide from his worried gaze, but I can't move. He reaches forward slowly and pushes a strand of wet hair out of my face before closing the gap. I don't budge, just close my eyes as he shifts closer.

His arms slide around my body and I surprise myself as I lean my head against his chest. His heart beats faster and he wraps his arms around me, pulling me into an embrace. He's warm and strong and I slide my arms around him to hug him back. I haven't been hugged in so long. Not like this. I squeeze him tighter as I cry, very aware of the fact that I'm soaking the front of his shirt.

I know I need someone to fill the void Lucas left. Someone to let me cry, to talk me through things. Someone to make me feel like I'm somebody and not just a shadow of my former self. Carson is that person. Even if I haven't known him very long, I feel safe with him. Comfortable. He's a friend. And that's enough for now.

I'm not sure how long we stand there but finally I pull away. There's a huge wet spot on his shirt but he doesn't seem to care. I wipe my eyes with the back of my hand and take a shaky breath. "I'm sorry . . . about that," I say. My voice is hoarse. I feel a little better and a lot worse. My head hurts and my eyes sting. After being dunked in the ocean and having an emotional breakdown, I'm sure I'm a mess.

"No, *I'm* sorry. For yelling at you." He sighs. "I overreacted."

"No, you didn't. I deserved it."

I feel him watching me, so I glance up. "I'm sorry about your brother."

"Don't be sorry. It's not your fault he's gone." I know that's not what he means but this has been my automatic response when anyone says it.

"What happened?"

I sigh and sit in one of the wicker chairs on the porch. Carson takes the other, never taking his eyes off me. "He was diagnosed with osteosarcoma when he was eighteen."

He raises an eyebrow.

"Bone cancer," I say. "We thought he had a good diagnosis at first. It was just in his femur. But then they found it other places as well. After a year of chemo, he stopped treatments and they only gave him a few months. He died a few weeks ago."

He looks at the ground. "I'm so sorry."

"My mom thought it would be a good idea to get away from everything for a while, so we moved here until summer starts." I let out another shaky breath. "We might be here for a while now though. My parents are getting divorced."

"I know how that is. It's not fun."

"Your parents are divorced?"

132

He nods. "They divorced when I was ten. My birth mom left us and my dad remarried my 'mom' two years later. I was young but I still remember everything about all of it. Every fight my parents had, every emotion I felt the day my mom left. It was harder on me than I'd like to admit. It still is, since I haven't seen her since. Sometimes the sadness creeps in now and then, but I'm human. You can't expect to block everything bad out. You wouldn't be able to appreciate the good otherwise. You know?"

I stare at the ground and nod. He's right.

"Anyway, we can talk about them later. I want to hear about you."

"Oh." I don't want to talk about just me, but it might make me feel better to talk to someone about it. "Well . . . I'm not surprised about the divorce. Not really. My mom is a control freak and does what she wants when she wants. She's never been very good at compromising or communicating really. I'd call her personality more cold than anything. She was different before Lucas got sick, but now . . ." I shake my head. "My dad is more laid back but likes things his way too. You can imagine what they were like when Lucas was diagnosed. They both wanted different treatments and opinions from different doctors. It was a nightmare. Lucas finally just told them what he was going to do, and since it was his life, they had to let him decide."

"You were close to him, weren't you." It isn't a question

"He was my best friend." Tears fill my eyes again and I blink furiously to push them back. I've dealt with enough emotions today. I don't want to look weak but it's exactly how I feel. "I know some siblings don't get along but it wasn't like that with us. He even left me a notebook full of letters when he died. To make sure I'd be okay. . . . But I'm not." I wipe at my wet cheeks. "Sorry. I'm usually not like this."

"It's okay to let it all out," Carson says.

"I hate it." I attempt to dry my eyes and sniff. "My parents made me talk to a counselor at the hospital and she always said the same thing."

"Really?"

"Yes. It was sort of like a class. The hospital offers it for free when you have a sibling with cancer. It's basically to let you know your parents love you still even though they spend so much time with said sibling and blah blah blah. Anyway, my counselor was always surprised I never cried at our sessions. I just hate crying though." I really need a tissue. My head feels like it might explode if I don't blow my nose soon.

He reaches over and takes my hand. "Thank you for telling me about Lucas. I wish I could have met him."

I sniff. "You remind me of him a little. Maybe that's why I get along with you so well."

He smiles and gives my hand a squeeze.

I sniff again and take a deep breath. "Do you want to come inside? I really need to blow my nose." I'm mortified I said it but he doesn't laugh. He just nods and helps me out of my chair.

Once we're inside, I all but run to the bathroom. I avoid looking in the mirror at first but sneak a peek after my sinuses are cleared. I look like a monster. My face is pale with blotches of red on my cheeks and around my eyes. I know I'm an ugly crier but this is ridiculous. I splash some cold water on my face, not sure if it will do anything. I've just seen it in movies so many times it seems the right thing to do. After I clean up, I go back in my room.

Carson is sitting on the floor, leaning against my bed with my guitar case on his lap. "Will teaching me how to play the guitar cheer you up at all? I'm sure I'll screw it up enough to make you laugh."

I let out a light chuckle and sit down next to him. "Now is as good a time as any."

He runs his fingers lightly across my cheek. "You have a beautiful smile. You should smile more often."

My cheeks heat and I focus on opening my guitar to distract myself from the really hot boy sitting next to me. The really hot boy who likes to touch me, hold my hand, compliment my work, and hang out with me. This is unreal.

"Your case is cool," he says.

I glance at the worn band stickers. The black case is barely visible underneath. I've been collecting them since my freshman year. A few of them are so worn out I can't even tell what band they were. "Thanks."

My guitar looks the same as it did the last time I played it. Old, but perfect. I pull it out and run my fingers over the shiny wood. I haven't played since the night before Lucas died. The last time he was awake. He told me over and over there was something comforting about it and always asked me to play for him, especially at night. Music helped him sleep and I still remember the peaceful look on his face as he listened to me play.

"You okay?" Carson asks.

"Yes. It's just . . ." I slide my fingers down the strings but don't strum them. "The last time I played this was the night Lucas died. He always liked to hear me play and wanted that to be the last thing he heard." I play with one of the strings. "I'm trying to talk myself into playing again."

"You don't have to if it's too painful."

I shake my head. "I do. I need to keep living my life. I can't keep avoiding things that remind me of him." I take my tuner out of my case and tune the strings. They sound pretty bad and I don't put the tuner back until I'm satisfied. I strum a chord and smile. My fingers know right where to go and I close my eyes, take a deep breath, and play one of my favorite classical pieces—Prelude from Bach's Cello Suite No. 1. It's difficult, but gorgeous and so worth all the hours I practiced to perfect it. The music flows from my fingertips and I forget myself for a moment. All I can feel is the music. I forgot how powerful it can be.

"You play beautifully," Carson says.

I open my eyes and feel my cheeks heat. "Thanks." I stop playing and hand him the guitar. "You're sure you want me to teach you? I'm not the best guitarist in the world."

"Who is?" he says. "You sound pretty good to me. And it doesn't matter who teaches me. I'm gonna suck anyway."

"You don't know that," I say. "But you might suck for a while." He laughs as I scoot closer to him. Our legs and shoulders touch and at first I tense up but then I made myself relax. "Hold it like this." I show him. "Put the strap around your neck. Left hand on the guitar's neck, right hand near the sound hole where the strings are."

He moves his hands and smiles. "Like this?"

"Yep. You'll strum with your right hand and your left hand will push down different strings on the fret board. Now lean against the bed. If you lean forward, you'll get really uncomfortable fast."

He leans back and then looks at me with a strange expression. "What's a fret board?"

I chuckle. "You see those little metal strips under the strings?"

He looks down at them and nods.

"Those are frets. If you push anywhere between the frets, you change the notes you're playing."

"Huh. Sorry, I don't know anything about the guitar."

"Um . . . have you seen me surf? Obviously I have no idea what I'm doing either."

"Yes you do. You did fine." He frowns. "Besides today."

"I know. I was stupid." I don't want to talk about it again so I shake my head. "Anyway, here's a guitar pick. Hold it like this." I touch his hand and turn the palm toward his body. "There. Perfect."

He raises an eyebrow. "Really?"

"Yes." My face is super close to his so I look away and focus on his hand instead. "Hold on tight to the pick and strum the strings like this." I move his hand up and down and let go as he does it himself. "Your upward strokes should sound the same as your downward strokes."

"They're . . . sort of the same."

It buzzes as he strums upward, but the more he does it, the better it sounds. "This is pretty easy."

"Well, of course that part's easy. We need to work on your fretting hand now." I point at his left hand and smile.

"You mean I actually have to do something with this hand?"

"Uh . . . yes. Let's start with a G chord."

It's been about an hour and Carson has mastered "Mary Had a Little Lamb." He plays it again with a huge smile on his face. "I should go play at a preschool or something."

"I'm sure those kids would love it."

He laughs and pulls the strap from around his neck and hands the guitar to me. "I'd rather hear *you* play something. I'm sure you've mastered every nursery rhyme in the book."

I shrug. "Yeah, probably." I giggle and play something he might recognize.

"No way! Love 'Stairway to Heaven,'" he says. He leans over, watching my fingers as I play the intro. He surprises me and starts singing when I reach the first verse. I'm tempted to sing along but I know he'll probably run screaming from the room if I do, so I just nod my head along with the beat.

I finish the song and look over at him. "You have a good voice."

"Eh. It's alright." He leans close to me and points at one of the notes. "So, how did you play this song again? Is it too hard for me to learn?"

"Yeah . . . probably. Let's start with something easier. Why don't you strum and I'll play the frets. We'll make up our own song."

He chuckles, scoots closer, and sets his hand behind me. He reaches across me and waits with his guitar pick to strum the strings. I try to stay focused but it's hard knowing he's *right there.*

"You ready?" My voice shakes.

"Are you?" His breath tickles my ear and I'm very aware of how close we are. I turn my head ever so slightly and he's there, staring at me. My breath quickens and my heart beats faster. I know what's coming but I'm not sure if I'm ready. I've never kissed anyone. I've never even been close. My heart hammers in my chest as I try to calm myself down.

It's a lost cause.

He leans close enough that I feel his breath on my lips. My eyes close and even though my mind is screaming at me to stop it before it happens, I don't. I can't. It's a perfect moment. His lips touch mine for just a moment before he pulls away. I open my eyes and he looks at me as though he's asking if it's okay. I stare at him and he hesitates only a second before leaning in again, his lips soft and gentle on mine. His hand slides up my back, his other one cradles my cheek. Part of me feels like melting into a puddle and the other is worried I'm doing something wrong.

Too soon he pulls away again, his eyes never leaving mine. He frowns when he sees my face. "I'm sorry," he says. "I didn't . . . I'm sorry."

I shake my head. "Don't be sorry. I've just never . . . you know." I blush. "I've never kissed anyone before. I've never . . . well, dated anyone either. Obviously. Since I haven't kissed anyone." I squeeze my eyes shut and chuckle at the nonsense spewing from my mouth. I don't know why I'm telling him any of this. I'm really wishing I'd shut up but I'm so nervous that I can't focus on anything.

He smiles. "Don't worry. I couldn't tell at all."

I put my guitar down in its case and fold my arms. The silence is making me anxious. I can't look at him. I'm not sure what the proper etiquette is after you kiss someone, so I just sit there staring at the floor. He must be reading my thoughts again because he reaches for my hand. He gives it a squeeze and stands, pulling me up with him. "I'd better go. You've had a rough day, and my dad wants me back at the shop tonight. I have to do some inventory for the next few days."

That doesn't sound fun at all. For me or him. "Well, thanks for . . . you know. Being here. With me." My cheeks heat yet again. I know our relationship has changed now that we've kissed. At least it has to me. It makes me worried. And excited. And terrified. And a little guilty. I shouldn't be falling for some guy when I'm supposed to be mourning my brother. And my parents' marriage.

"You can talk to me any time. You know that, right?"

I nod. It's strange to think back on the last few weeks. I still don't know him very well but I feel like we've been friends forever. "I know." I walk him to the door. "Have fun at work."

He pulls me into a hug and leans back. I wonder if he's going to kiss me again but he just smiles. "I'll call you later, okay?" He leans in and touches his lips to my forehead before leaving me by myself.

I'm flustered. I just kissed a guy I barely know. How do I feel about that? How do I feel about *him*? I know I like him or I wouldn't have let him kiss me, but now everything's going to be different. I sit on my bed and stare at the wall. The kiss replays in my head, over and over again. I smile and curl into a ball on top of my bedspread. I'm pretty sure I'm going to have good dreams tonight.

CHAPTER 13

DEAR OAKLEY,

SO SORRY ABOUT THE LAST LETTER. I WAS OUT OF SORTS. I'VE BEEN WATCHING TOO MUCH HARRY POTTER I THINK. OR MAYBE NO ONE IN HARRY POTTER SAYS THAT. DO OLD PEOPLE SAY IT? MERLIN'S BEARD, I'M A STRANGE ONE!

YOU HAVE NO IDEA HOW HARD I'M LAUGHING RIGHT NOW, WRITING THIS. THE NURSES PROBABLY THINK I'VE GONE CRAZY. THEY'RE PROBABLY RIGHT.

ANYWAY, REMEMBER WHEN WE WENT TO HARRY POTTER 5 THE DAY IT CAME OUT? AND THERE WAS AN OLD NASTY-LOOKING COUCH SITTING NEAR THE FRONT OF THE LINE WE WERE WAITING IN AND WE ACTUALLY SAT ON IT? AND EVERYONE WHO SAW US ASKED IF IT WAS OURS AND WE SAID YES? THAT WAS FUN. SERIOUSLY. HILARIOUS. EVEN THOUGH WE PROBABLY HAVE SOME KIND OF DISEASE FROM SITTING ON IT.

WE HAD SOME GOOD TIMES, DIDN'T WE? DON'T STOP DOING STUFF LIKE THAT. IT MAKES FOR GOOD STORIES AND FUN MEMORIES. KEEP MAKING MEMORIES, OAKLEY. YOU'LL REGRET IT IF YOU DON'T.

LOVE, LUCAS

We did have some good times. Too many to count. The Harry Potter memory was one of my favorites, though. Sitting outside in the sun and baking on that old couch. We were the first ones in line for that showing on opening day. I didn't want to be first but Lucas made me get out of the car and run to save our spot. It was embarrassing at the time but after it was pretty cool. There was even some tall guy dressed up as Hagrid who we took a picture with. We were super lame. But it was one of the best days.

"Oakley?"

I slide my notebook under my pillow as Jo opens the door. Her wild hair is pulled into a ponytail and she's standing in really short shorts and a tank top. If I had a body like hers, I'd wear that too. "Hey," I say.

She comes in and sits on the edge of my bed. "I just wanted you to know that your mom is picking your dad up at the airport this morning."

I freeze. "What?"

He really came? Were they working things out? Or did he bring divorce papers for her to sign? Can they get papers that fast?

Jo must see the panic on my face because she pats my hand. "I'm sorry she didn't tell you. It was very last minute for your dad to come visit. I actually argued with your mom to tell you herself but she didn't want to wake you this morning. They'll be back later, I promise."

"Okay." I have to hope they can work things out. I have to. Hope is the only thing I have left.

"Hey, it's gonna be okay," Jo says. She smiles, the creases near her eyes more pronounced than I remember. "I actually wanted to talk to you about something. I just received a call from the Coast Guard saying there's a sea lion in distress about ten minutes from here. Do you want to come with me to check it out? You can see what I do and get out of the house for a while. Your parents should be here by the time we come home."

"Sure." It's not like I have anything else to do. Carson's working anyway. "Let me change really quick."

"Great. Don't forget sunscreen this time." She points at my nose. "You're starting to peel a little."

Yep, *great*.

Fifteen minutes later, we're outside. I'm surprised to see Dillon waiting by Jo's truck. His face lights up when he sees me.

"How've you been? Haven't seen you for a few days."

"I'm good." He smells like coconuts again. "What are you doing here?"

"My dad works with Jo so he makes me help out now and then." He shrugs.

"Oh." We climb in Jo's truck as another one pulls up by ours. Jo sticks her head out the window and talks to the man and before I know it, we're following him down the street.

I sit next to Jo, who's talking loudly on her cell, and Dillon plops down next to me. He's wearing a really tight shirt and I can't help but check him out. He's ripped, that's for sure. A six-pack and everything. Carson has one too but he's not as tan. And his arms aren't as . . . shiny.

Dillon sees me looking and smiles, showing off his straight white teeth. He leans close to my ear. "You can keep looking. I don't mind."

He's super full of himself too.

I roll my eyes and look away.

"What?" he asks, laughing.

I'm thankful I don't have to answer since Jo is slowing the truck down. She pulls onto the beach and drives down to the water. "There she is," she says.

I look ahead and see a mass of brown lying on the sand with half its body in the water. The sea lion is barely moving and is making an awful noise. There's a group of people surrounding it but no one goes too close.

Dillon jumps out of the truck with Jo. I stay where I am, my eyes glued to the animal struggling in the water. I watch as a few men jump out of the other truck with big nets and other equipment. The sea lion doesn't move as they cover it.

I get out of the truck and walk over to where everyone is gathered, curious. I see Jo inject the animal with something in a really long needle, and Dillon strokes its head. But I don't look at its head for long. I stare at a mass of fat and bone sticking out of three deep gashes in its side. There isn't really any blood, just tissue and flesh.

I shudder to think about what must have happened and what kind of pain the animal is in. It just lies there, its breathing shallow.

"Oakley," Dillon says. "Why don't you go back to the truck?"

I don't answer, just stare. I can't tear my gaze away from the wound and after a moment, Dillon puts his arm around my shoulder and attempts to turn me around. To shield the animal from my view, I'm sure. "No, I'm okay. I want to see this." I turn back around, curious as to what they're going to do with it.

He raises an eyebrow. "You're sure?"

"Yes." I keep my distance but watch as Jo and her team go to work. Jo's obviously done this a million times. She's amazingly gentle and calm. She talks to the sea lion like it's a person as they load it into some kind of stretcher, petting its head and making sure it's comfortable. My fingers itch to touch it as well. To comfort it somehow.

"Looks like she got hit by a boat," Dillon says.

I glance at him for a moment. I'd forgotten he was even there. The sea lion makes another awful noise. It tugs at my heart. "What's going to happen to her?"

Dillon frowns. "She's in pretty bad shape. From what I've seen, and I'm not a vet or anything, but the injury is probably gonna do her in. I doubt she even makes it back to the rescue center."

"How . . . sad."

He shrugs. "There are plenty of sea lions around. Sad to see them go like this but that's the circle of life, I guess."

I crack a smile. "You're not gonna start singing *The Lion King* are you?"

He grins. "You want me to?"

"Not really."

He chuckles and is quiet for a minute. "So, you and Carson, huh?"

I glance at him, surprised. "What?"

"You're a thing now?"

I look away. "I'm not sure what you mean."

"Oh, come on. I talked to him this morning." There's tension in his voice and he looks away, suddenly examining something beyond us.

"We're friends."

He laughs. "Friends. Right."

"You okay, Oakley?"

I look up, grateful to see Jo. Her clothes are soaking wet and she uses her arm to push a clump of hair out of her face. "I'm fine," I say. "You're amazing."

She rolls her eyes. "Not really. And I'm sorry you had to see that. We don't get a lot of sea lions that are still alive after an accident like this. This one's a fighter. I don't think she's going to make it though. The wound is too severe."

I nod, feeling my chest tighten. The poor animal. "I'm sorry."

She shrugs. "It happens. Way too often for my liking though." She slips her arm through mine. "Let's get back to the rescue center and you can go do what you want. I feel bad I made you come with me. You shouldn't have to see this."

"It's okay, Jo. I'm really glad I came. What you do for the animals is really awesome. I'd like to come again another time, if you don't mind."

She looks surprised but nods anyway. "Of course I don't mind. I'd love to have you around." I smile at her and she pats me on the back before walking away.

I follow Dillon to the truck and we get inside.

"Your aunt's pretty cool," he says. "She's rescued a lot of animals. Have you been to the rescue center yet?"

I shake my head. Dillon is back to his old self. The tension between us seems to be gone.

"You'll have to come inside when we get there. It's nice." He stretches his arms behind his head and closes his eyes.

We wait until they load the animal in the truck and then we're off. We reach the rehabilitation center quickly. Jo drives the truck up a long driveway, goes around the building, and parks near a back door.

A whole bunch of people come running out of the building and Jo and Dillon help them take the sea lion inside. I don't know what to do so I sit in the truck until Jo returns. As she pokes her head out of the building, she asks, "You doin' okay?"

"Yes."

"Why don't you come inside? I'll show you around. There are a lot of happier stories in here."

I jump out and follow her through the doors. Just seeing this one part of the building, I know the rest is huge. Large cages with seals and sea lions are everywhere.

Some swim happily in their pools, others relax on the sides. The pools look like normal swimming pools but I know they're filled with salt water. And freezing cold, I'm sure.

I peek into the closest pen and see a sea lion lying on the side near the gate. It has a huge bite mark in its skin. It's not as bad as the one I saw on the beach but it still looks awful. It looks up as we walk by and moves away to slide into the pool of water in its pen.

Jo stops at one particular gate and smiles. "This is Benny. I found him when he was just a pup. He was severely dehydrated and sick. We couldn't locate his mother, so we brought him here. She probably died, since sea lions don't usually leave their pups for very long." She leans down and smiles at the sea lion. "He's doing well enough now that we're going to release him next week. It's always bittersweet." She gives him one last look and continues walking.

There are so many animals here. Seals, sea lions, a few dolphins. It's amazing how much Jo and her team do for them.

"I need to check on that female we brought in earlier." She studies me. "You can sit in my office if you want or you can come with me. It's up to you."

I shrug. "I'll come with you."

"You're sure?"

I nod. I can't explain why I want to see it again. The fact that it's dying is sad, and it does bother me, but what if I could do something like this? What if I could save animals from the fate that this sea lion is going to suffer?

Jo walks through a hallway and past a few doors. She goes into a white room where a bunch of people surround the hurt animal. "How's she doing?"

One of the vets, I assume, looks her in the eye. "We're going to have to put her down. She's not going to make it."

Jo sighs and pats the guy on the back. "It's been a bad few months, hasn't it? I wish we could train the animals to stay away from boats, but alas." She frowns. "Let's not let her suffer anymore. And if it's okay with you, I'm going to take my niece out of here."

"I'm really—" I want to tell Jo I'm fine but she's already pulling me out the door.

"I'll take care of her," he says. He gives me a sad smile and turns back around.

Jo looks past him at the sea lion on the table and lets out another sigh.

"Come on, Oakley. You don't want to see this part." She turns and grabs my hand, pulling me out of the room.

"She's going to die then?"

She nods. "There's too much trauma. She's not responding and her heart rate is very low. It's a miracle she made it this long."

"Like you said earlier. She's a fighter." I look back at the closed door, wishing I could comfort the creature before she dies.

"Yes, she is. We're able to rescue most of the animals we bring in but there are a few who don't make it." She runs a hand through her messy curls. "I wish boaters would pay closer attention to their surroundings. This happens way too often. Sometimes when the sea lions are under the water there's no way you can see them, but all too often the driver just isn't paying attention."

I fold my arms across my chest as she leads me back the way we came. Dillon is waiting for us. "My dad called. He should be here in about ten minutes. They found a dolphin stranded on Newport Beach and he wants you to go with him."

"Can you take Oakley home? This one will probably take a while."

He looks at me and smiles. "Sure."

"I'll be home later, Oakley. I have my cell if you need me."

"Okay." I watch her pull out her cell and walk away quickly. I frown and look at Dillon. "Wait. Didn't you ride with us this morning? How are we gonna get home?"

He produces some car keys and dangles them in front of my face. "Dad always has an extra car here."

"Oh. Well, that's convenient."

He smiles. "Shall we?" He leads me out the door and to the parking lot. I don't know a lot about cars but his is super nice. Like, really nice. I'm sure Lucas would know what it is but all I know is its really shiny and black.

I'm quiet as Dillon drives. I feel weird around him. He always seems to bring up Carson and it's not any of his business what I do in my free time.

"So, how long are you gonna be here again?" He looks over at me as he drives.

"Until April or May. My mom said we'd be leaving before summer starts."

"Why are you here anyway?"

I sigh. "It's a long story."

"You were just looking to meet me, right?" He laughs at the expression I give him.

"That's exactly it," I say. Not really. I am, however, very glad I met Carson. I wonder if he's off work yet.

I change the subject. "Do you always go with Jo when she has a rescue?"

He shakes his head. "Only sometimes. Carson goes more than me. He actually enjoys it. But he works at the surf shop a lot more than I do so he can't go as often as he'd like. When he can't go, I fill in. Sometimes we go together but usually Jo only wants one of us."

"You don't like to go?"

"It's not that I don't like it, I'd just rather be surfing. My dad's a vet, so he's trying to pass on his love of animals to me." He shrugs. "Not in my world. I like animals well enough but that's not what I'm going to do for the rest of my life. He's cool with it. At least he says he is. Not like Carson's old man. He's pretty set on controlling Carson's future. Been that way since we were in middle school."

"Oh." Poor Carson. "So, what do you want to do if you're not going to be a vet then?"

He shrugs. "Not sure. I have all the time in the world to figure it out though. I'm hoping I can move to Hawaii. I have relatives over there."

"I've never been."

"Me neither. Yet."

I think about what I want to do when I get back to Utah. Everything there seems like it's so in the past. If I can get a little braver, working with Jo would be really awesome. She seems to love it. And I love animals. It would be hard to see some of the ones I'd have to rescue but if I can help them in any way, it might be worth it. I'll have to talk to her and see how hard it is to go into her field. Maybe it will be easier if I know her. I'd sort of have an in.

Dillon pulls into my driveway and my eyes widen when I see Carson sitting on my front steps. He has a bunch of papers in his hands and looks up when he hears us. I swear he looks upset when he sees Dillon with me but he relaxes just as fast.

"Hey," I say, stepping out of the car.

"Your old man let you out early today?" Dillon asks.

Carson nods and stands. "We were a little slow so he said he'd stay and close."

"Good to know, bro." Dillon claps Carson on the back. "We've been out saving sea lions today."

He glances at me. "Jo took you to a rescue?"

I blush under his gaze. "Yes."

He studies me for a second and the corner of his mouth turns up. "Did you see the facility?"

I nod. "It was really cool. I can see why you want to go into that field."

Dillon laughs. "If you like that sort of thing. Anyway, we rescued a sea lion today. She was pretty messed up. Hit by a boat. They had to put her down."

"That's too bad," Carson says. He's still watching me, a strange expression on his face.

"Well, I've gotta get this car back or my dad will freak."

"Thanks for the ride," I say.

He winks, which freaks me out a little. "Anytime. We should do it again. Soon." He climbs into his car and drives away.

I turn and face Carson, who's still looking at me. "What?"

"Nothing." He looks away and sits back down on the porch steps. "I was just looking through these college applications. I'm not sure what to put down for my major."

He has college applications? I wonder if his dad knows. "When are they due?"

"The end of March, so I only have a couple weeks left to mail them in."

"I thought you wanted to be a veterinarian?"

"I do."

I frown. "Then why don't you write it down?"

He sighs. "You know why." He frowns. "If my dad sees anything but business or accounting or something on here, he'd flip."

"But you don't want to go into those things."

He closes his eyes and shakes his head, rubbing at his temples. "My mom's on board but he's so stubborn. He'll never change his mind about this."

I sigh and put my hand on his arm. "He can't control your life."

He frowns. "You don't know him like I do."

"Well, no, but it's *your* life. He should support whatever you want to do."

"It's not that simple."

"It *is* that simple. He should at least give you his blessing."

He stands suddenly. "He won't. I already know what he'll say. He's already said it before. It all comes down to the same thing. The stupid shop. That's all he cares about. He won't help me out if I go into something else. And there's no way I can afford to go without his help."

"Have you talked to him about how you feel about being a veterinarian? *Really* talked to him about it? Or do you just drop it altogether when he says something?"

He clenches his jaw and doesn't say anything. His whole body is tense and, by the way he's acting, I have a feeling he's mad at not only his dad, but me as well. I don't know what I've done to make him angry though.

"Talk to him. Tell him what you're going to do and just do it. I'm sure he'll come around."

"I've tried," he snaps.

"Maybe you should try harder." I shut my mouth. I shouldn't be giving him advice when I can't even talk to Mom.

I shrink under his glare, thinking he's going to yell at me, but he doesn't. He just takes a step back and looks at the papers in his hand again. "You know, I'm tired. I should go." He doesn't look at me, doesn't say goodbye, just walks back to his house. I stare after him until he goes in and slams the door behind him.

What just happened?

CHAPTER 14

I go straight to my room. As usual, I read a letter from Lucas to make me feel better.

DEAR OAKLEY,

HAVE YOU EVER WONDERED WHAT HEAVEN LOOKS LIKE? I HAVE. I'VE HEARD IT'S BEAUTIFUL. PEACEFUL. I'M HOPING IT'S TRUE. I DON'T THINK I COULD DEAL WITH UNICORNS AND RAINBOWS OR SOMETHING WEIRD LIKE THAT.

I WONDER IF THEY PLAY BASKETBALL THERE. THAT WOULD BE ALL KINDS OF AWESOME. YOU SHOULD PICTURE ME PLAYING BASKETBALL WHEN THERE'S A THUNDERSTORM. THE THUNDER WOULD PROBABLY BE ME SWEARING THOUGH . . . HA HA.

I HOPE IT'S WARM. WITH LOTS OF SUNSHINE AND TREES AND GRASS. GREEN. ALIVE. A PLACE I CAN BE CONTENT AND HAPPY. PARADISE.

LOVE, LUCAS

I reread the letter several times. Not because it doesn't make sense, but because Lucas seemed to have it all figured out before he died. I hope he's playing basketball every day.

The front door opens and I put Lucas's notebook away before going to see who's home. Dad sees me first and I run to him. He picks me up in his big arms and squeezes me tight. He smells like he's had a cappuccino. I love that smell.

"I've missed you," he says. He sets me down and looks me over. "You look too skinny. Has Jo been feeding you?"

I laugh. "I haven't even been here long enough to starve, Dad. And Jo's feeding me just fine."

"Good."

Mom appears behind him and gives me a small smile before going in the kitchen and pouring herself a glass of water.

Dad sits down on Jo's couch and pats the cushion next to him. "Tell me about surfing. I want to know how you managed to learn something as cool as that."

I tell him. About everything. Surfing, Carson—making sure to leave the kissing part out, of course—the whales, going to Jo's work. It's just like it used to be. He listens and laughs. It's like he's been here with us the whole time. Like nothing's changed. We sit there for what seems like hours. It takes me a while to realize something's missing.

"Where's Mom?" I ask and look around.

Dad shrugs and glances at his watch. "She's tired, I think."

"Oh." Just when I was starting to feel like I belonged to a normal family, she disappears. Did she want to leave us alone? Or was she avoiding Dad?

Dad taps his fingers on his knee and glances at his watch again.

"Do you have somewhere to be?" I ask.

He smiles, though I can tell it's forced. "I do, actually. My flight leaves in a few hours."

"What?" I look around and notice he has no luggage with him. "You're not staying?"

He shakes his head. "I just came here to see you. I wanted to see how you're doing. Mom told you what's going on, I'm sure."

I nod and swallow the sudden lump in my throat. "You're getting divorced." So it's really happening then. And I had the false hope that they were going to work things out. Like in that movie, *The Parent Trap*, I used to watch as a kid.

He closes his eyes and rubs a hand over them. "We can't fix this, Oakley. We're both broken. We care about each other, of course, but it's not enough to save our marriage. It's for the best."

"Have you even tried to work it out? Have you talked about it? I'm sure there's something—"

"I'm sorry, pumpkin." He grabs my hand and squeezes it. The look on his face says it all. He's done trying.

I look down at our hands. "Why did you even come here then?"

"I wanted to make sure you were okay."

"You could have called instead of wasting your time and money."

"I'm not wasting my time. I want to make sure you're okay with this. And to see if you like it here. If you don't . . . I mean . . . if you'd like to come back home with me, you're more than welcome."

I stare at him. "You want me to live with you instead of Mom?"

He nods. "If you'd like. You're almost eighteen, so you can make your own decision. All your stuff is where it was before you left. You can come back with me right now and things will be like they were before."

I smile a little even though I know he's wrong. Things will never be like they were before. Not without Lucas, and not without Mom. His offer is tempting. Part of me wants to go home. I haven't even seen Lucas's headstone yet, and to be honest, I miss my little town. But another part of me wants to stay. I like it here. I like hanging out with Jo and being with Carson. And I know I need to work things out with Mom. Fix the rift that has come between us. I can't leave. Not yet.

"You don't want to leave," he says. He gives me a sad smile. "I can see it in your eyes. You like it here."

"It's not that, Dad. I just . . ." I sigh. "It's just different. And I need different right now."

He squeezes my hand again and stands. "I understand." And by the look on his face, I really think he's telling the truth. He looks at his watch again. "I've got to get going. Don't want to miss that flight. I have to be at work bright and early."

Work. It's always about work. He holds his arms open and I go to him. He hugs me tight and I know I'm probably breaking his heart by not leaving with him. It makes me sad to think of him alone in the house with all of our things.

"Thanks for coming to see me, Dad. It's not the same without you here."

He smiles. "I wish I could stay longer, but I'm glad I came. And you are welcome home anytime. You know that, right?"

"Of course. I love you."

"I love you, too." We hug again as Mom walks into the room.

"You ready to go?" she asks. Her voice is cold as she addresses him and my heart aches. I hate seeing them like this but there's nothing I can do.

He lets go of me and nods. "Yes."

"Let's get going." She looks at me. "Jo should be home any minute, Oakley. I'll be back in an hour or so."

"Okay."

Dad follows her to the door, gives me another one of his sad smiles, and shuts the door behind him.

I stare at the door for a long time, wondering if I've done the right thing.

CHAPTER 15

DEAR OAKLEY,

SOMETIMES PEOPLE SUCK. LIKE THAT ONE TIME WHEN I LEFT MY WALLET AT THAT RESTAURANT AND SOMEONE STOLE IT. THEY COULD HAVE BEEN NICE AND GIVEN IT TO A SERVER, BUT NO. THEY TOOK IT HOME AND STOLE MY TWENTY BUCKS. I HAD TO GO THE STUPID DMV AND GET A NEW LICENSE. THAT WAS FUN. I THOUGHT I'D NEVER HEAR THE END OF IT FROM MOM. AND TODAY, SOMEONE STOLE MY SNICKERS OFF MY LUNCH TRAY. I THINK IT WAS MY NEW NURSE. SHE HAS IT OUT FOR ME, AND I SWEAR I COULD SMELL CHOCOLATE ON HER BREATH WHEN SHE CAME IN EARLIER.

I REALLY WANTED THAT SNICKERS. EAT A FEW FOR ME, OKAY? EVEN THOUGH I KNOW YOU LIKE MILKY WAYS BETTER. AT LEAST EAT ONE SNICKERS FOR ME. I'LL MISS THEM.

LOVE, LUCAS

It's late. Like 2 a.m. late. I set Lucas's notebook back on the nightstand and lie back on my bed. I've tossed and turned for hours and can't sleep. I can't stop thinking about Dad's offer. I know he misses me, and I miss him, but something is keeping me here. I decide not to dwell on it and think about my other problem: my earlier conversation with Carson. It replays over and over in my head. He was mad and it's my fault. I know I shouldn't have told him to talk to his dad. It wasn't my place to say anything like that.

I have to apologize.

I know it's stupid but I sneak out of my room. Maybe he's awake like me. And if not, I'll figure something out. I make it halfway to Carson's house and realize what I'm wearing. A white tank and bright pink board shorts. Nice. At least I'm wearing a bra, I guess.

I sneak around Carson's house and see a light coming from a basement window. I'm sure it's not his parents' room, since I've never met anyone whose parents sleep in the basement, so I take a chance and knock on it.

A few seconds later, the blinds open enough for me to see a pair of dark brown eyes. They don't belong to Carson.

I step back as the eyes stare at me and then the blinds close.

Crap. Now what? I don't want to knock on another window. Who knows how many people live in Carson's house? He's never told me how many siblings he has; I know of at least one sister. I hesitate and take a step to start back to my house when the window I knocked on opens, spilling light onto me and my awesome pajamas.

"Oakley?" Carson stands in the room in just a pair of boxers. He looks tired.

"Uh . . . hi," I say. Now I'm embarrassed. Why the heck did I think it would be okay to knock on his window in the middle of the night?

He looks me over and a small smile appears. "What are you doing?"

I fold my arms. "I couldn't sleep. And . . . I needed to talk to you."

"Now?" He smiles wider. "At two in the morning?"

"I know. I'm an idiot."

He laughs. "No, you're not. Hold on a sec."

"Oh, just let her in. I want to meet her anyway," another voice says.

A face appears over his shoulder. A tall girl with big brown eyes and a dark complexion.

Carson comes over to the window again. "Come on," he says and reaches a hand toward me. I step down onto the sill and his strong hands wrap around my arms to help me inside.

He doesn't release me when my feet are on the floor and I put a hand on his chest. I try not to stare at him, especially with another person in the room, but it's hard not to. He looks amazing.

I clear my throat and step back. His cheeks turn pink and he motions toward the girl standing behind him. "Oakley, this is Keilani. My sister."

I remember hearing her name. They don't look anything alike though. She looks Polynesian or something.

She's beautiful, with perfect skin and straight black hair. That's when I remember Carson's dad remarried. Of course they don't look alike. They're step-siblings.

She moves forward and pulls me into a hug. I'm too surprised to say anything, so I awkwardly hug her back. She squeezes me really tight before letting go. "I've been wanting to meet you since Carson first told me about you."

I glance at him and he looks away, embarrassed. "What has he told you exactly?"

"That we're the same age. Isn't that wonderful?" She laughs and brushes her long dark hair out of her face. "I wish you weren't already graduated though. We could totally hang out at school."

"Yeah, I lucked out on that, I guess. I forget people are still in school around here. It just feels like a long summer vacation for me."

She chuckles. "Seriously. Lucky. I still have three months until I graduate." She frowns, then her eyes light up again. "Carson told me you play the guitar too. I'd love to hear you sometime."

I glance at Carson as he beams down at me. "Oh, come on. I'm not *that* good."

Carson nudges me. "Whatever." He chuckles. "She sings too. Apparently just about as good as you, Lani."

Her eyes widen. "You can't sing either?"

I laugh. "Nope. Thanks for bringing that up by the way." I look over at him and smile. We stare at each other a moment until Keilani clears her throat.

"I'll . . . uh . . . leave you two alone." She giggles and starts to leave the room.

"This is your room, Lani. We'll go in my room."

"I doubt Mom would like that," she says, giving him a look.

He rolls his eyes. "It's two in the morning, Lani. You know she's here. We're not gonna . . . get in trouble or anything."

I can't look at Carson. I know I'm red from head to toe.

She shrugs. "I'll be in the kitchen eating ice cream. Come get me when you're done 'talking.'" She winks at me and leaves us alone.

"She seems—"

"Crazy?" Carson finishes.

"I was going to say nice. People don't usually hug me. That was oddly comforting."

"Lani likes to hug people. I think it's weird, but whatever." He smiles and stares at me a second before running his fingers through his messy hair. "So, why'd you come over anyway?"

"I wanted to apologize. For earlier. I shouldn't have said anything about your dad. I'm sorry."

He raises his eyebrows. "You're apologizing to me?" He shakes his head. "I should be apologizing to you. I was a jerk. You didn't do anything wrong. It was just me being stupid."

"But I said you should talk to your dad. I shouldn't have said that when I have the same problem with my mom."

"You were right though. I should talk to him." He steps closer. "I was in a bad mood. I'm sorry I took it out on you." He heaves a sigh. "And then I saw you with Dillon and I just . . ." He trails off and looks away.

Oh. He saw me with Dillon. It all makes sense now. "You think I like Dillon?"

He shrugs. "I have no idea what to think. I know he's had a thing for you since he saw you on the beach that first day. And all the other girls seem to throw themselves in front of him whenever they get the chance. It wouldn't surprise me at all if you went after him."

I chuckle. It's hilarious that he's jealous and that he thinks I'd ever "go after" anyone. I have no desire to date Dillon at all. Especially when I just kissed Carson last night. Which we should probably talk about but I'm not brave enough to bring it up. "I don't like Dillon. Even a little bit."

He glances at me with a look of relief. "Really?"

"Really." I pause and smile. "He *is* pretty tan though," I say. "And the way his eyes match the ocean is dazzling."

Carson grins. "He has brown eyes."

"Oh. Oops. See? I don't even know what color eyes he has."

He takes a step toward me and slides his arms around my waist. "You're hilarious. And your outfit is really . . . cute."

"Cute?" I wrinkle my nose. Cute sounds like something a little girl would wear. "Should I put pigtails in my hair to match all this cuteness?"

167

He smiles before he leans in and whispers in my ear. "If you want me to say sexy, I will."

I chuckle and bury my face against his chest so he doesn't see me blush. "I think you should have stuck with cute," I say into his shirt.

"Sexy it is."

I half laugh, half snort, making my cheeks flame. He chuckles and holds me closer, making my heart speed up. We both grow quiet as I pull away just enough to meet his eyes, and before I know what's happening, his lips are on mine.

I'm not sure what to do again, since it's not just a little kiss, but my lips move on their own and his hands tighten around my waist. I slide my fingers up his arms and around his neck. I feel him smile underneath my lips and pull away.

"What?" I say. "Am I doing something wrong?"

He doesn't say anything, just shakes his head and kisses me again. I never knew how much fun kissing could be. And now that I know how it feels, I don't want it to end.

We pull away just as we hear someone coming down the stairs. I step away from Carson as Keilani bounds into the room.

"Enjoy your ice cream?" Carson asks, sneaking a glance at me.

"Yep. Now I'd like to go to bed, so you know, wrap it up." She gives me a smile. "It was so nice to meet you, Oakley. We'll have to hang out soon. I know we'll be great friends."

"Um, she was *my* friend first," Carson says.

She laughs. "Right. Friend," she says slowly.

I chuckle and head toward the window. Carson tells me goodnight and wraps me in a hug. "Thanks for coming over. I'm still sorry about today."

"Don't worry about it," I say. "I'll see you tomorrow."

He doesn't kiss me, just helps me back out the window. I break into a jog and make it back to my room in one piece.

I'm wired now. From the kiss, from Carson basically admitting he was jealous of Dillon, and from meeting Keilani. But mostly just from the kiss.

I'm pretty sure I *won't* sleep well tonight.

CHAPTER 16

DEAR OAKLEY,

    I HAD A REALLY WEIRD DREAM LAST NIGHT. WE WERE RUNNING THOUGH SOME FIELD AND PEOPLE WERE CHASING US WITH KNIVES AND STUFF. I WAS AN AWESOME ARCHER AND YOU WERE PRETTY COOL, TOO, THOUGH I CAN'T REMEMBER WHY. ALL I REMEMBER IS I WAS CRAZY AWESOME AND TOOK OUT LIKE TEN PEOPLE. I SAVED YOUR LIFE. YOU SHOULD BE PROUD OF ME THAT I CARED SO MUCH ABOUT MY BABY SISTER. EVEN THOUGH WE'RE TWO YEARS APART, YOU'RE STILL MY BEST FRIEND. BUT THAT DOESN'T CHANGE THE FACT THAT I'M STILL OLDER AND WISER THAN YOU. AND A LITTLE COOLER, I THINK. BUT YOU ALREADY KNOW THAT, DON'T YOU. AND NO, THAT WASN'T A QUESTION.

    YOU KNOW WHAT I WISH I WOULD HAVE DONE? I WISH I WOULD HAVE READ MORE BOOKS. YOU OF ALL PEOPLE KNOW HOW MUCH I DESPISE READING ANYTHING. MY EYES CAN'T HANDLE THAT MUCH STIMULATION. ACTUALLY, I JUST GET BORED. BESIDES THE HARRY POTTER BOOKS, AND THOSE REALLY "DEEP" BOOKS I HAD TO READ FOR HONORS ENGLISH THAT I NEVER UNDERSTOOD . . . OR FINISHED, I HAVEN'T REALLY READ ANYTHING. I'M SURE THERE ARE A LOT OF GOOD BOOKS OUT THERE.

SO DO ME A FAVOR AND READ SOME FOR ME. PROBABLY START WITH THE HUNGER GAMES, SINCE MY DREAM WAS BASICALLY ME AS KATNISS BUT MALE. THAT WAS A GOOD MOVIE. PROBABLY WOULD HAVE BEEN COOLER IF I HAD READ THE BOOKS FIRST. HAPPY HUNGER GAMES, OAKLEY. "AND MAY THE ODDS BE EVER IN YOUR FAVOR."

LOVE, LUCAS

Seven in the morning. Why am I awake so early? My head aches from being up so late and I set the notebook on the nightstand. I pick up my Kindle and download *The Hunger Games*. I've never read it and Lucas told me to, so I will. I set it back down on the nightstand and close my eyes again. I'll read it when I'm fully awake.

I hear Jo call my name from down the hall but put my pillow over my head instead. I don't want to get up yet. I'm exhausted. It's my own fault since I decided to go tap on people's windows in the middle of the night.

"Oakley!" Jo yells again.

"Too early," I say to myself. I pull my covers over my head as well.

She knocks on my door and opens it before I answer. "Oakley, I've been calling your name forever. Get up." She pulls the covers back but I don't move. I stay curled in my little ball in the middle of my bed.

"Can't I just have one more hour?" I squint at the light as she opens my blinds.

"I'm not gonna make that boy wait for you any longer, now get up."

I sit up and stare at her. "What boy?"

Her smile is cynical. "Carson's here. He says he's taking you surfing this morning."

"What?" I glance at the clock. It's a little past seven now. Mornings are seriously the worst.

She laughs at my expression this time. "Come on, Sleeping Beauty. He's already in his wet suit and everything. You'd better hurry and get dressed before he decides to take someone else."

Really? Who gets up this early when they don't have a reason to? I let out an exaggerated sigh and climb out of bed. My wet suit is in a heap on the floor in my closet, my swimsuit next to it. I put both of them on, though I'm not able to zip up the back of the suit.

One glance in the mirror on my wall and I'm freaking out. I look horrible. My eyes are all saggy and weird from lack of sleep and my hair is . . . well, let's just say it resembles some kind of wild animal. I dart across the hall to the bathroom, pat it down with some water, and pull it into a tight ponytail. I debate whether I should put on makeup. We're going surfing. In the ocean. I know it will all wash off but I slip on some foundation and a little mascara anyway.

Another glance in the mirror and my face looks a little better, but not much.

"Oakley? You ready yet?" Jo yells.

Taking one last look at my crappy self, I open the door and trudge down the hall.

"She almost takes as long as you. Which is saying something," Jo says. Carson laughs and I hear Mom laugh

172

as well. I come around the corner with my hands on my hips. Jo grins. "You heard that?"

"I'll never take as long as my mom does to get ready," I say. "What took me five minutes would be an hour for her."

Jo nods. "Yes. You're probably right."

Mom studies me for a second and looks at Jo. "Guilty."

Mom and I share a smile as Jo walks past me and into the kitchen. "Don't forget breakfast," she says, throwing me an apple.

"Thanks." I sink my teeth into it and take a big bite.

"You ready?"

I turn toward Carson. "Mmhmm." I'm surprised he hasn't run away yet. Or shrunk away at my appearance. I'm not lying when I say I look pretty bad. And now I'm chomping on an apple. Seriously. It's like half gone already.

"Let's go then," he says.

"Be careful, you two," Jo says as she pours some coffee in her mug.

"No worries," Carson says.

Mom hands me a towel. "Have fun."

I take it and meet her eyes, surprised by her smile. "We will." She hasn't talked to me about Dad's surprise visit yet, but there really isn't much to say. She knows I chose to stay with her, for whatever reason.

I grab my surfboard and follow Carson out the door. We cross the street and head down to the beach.

"Your mom's nice," he says.

"She's alright, I guess."

"She thinks a lot of you."

I glance at him. "Why do you say that?"

He shrugs. "She told me. You took a while getting ready and we talked."

"What did she say?" Do I want to know?

"She said you were really into sports when you were in high school and made the honor roll every term. She also told me you ran for senior class president and won. I didn't know that. That's pretty cool."

Was. Was cool. "She didn't mention the part when I dropped out of everything?"

He's silent for a moment. "No. She didn't mention that." He stops and grabs my hand. "She didn't say anything bad. Trust me."

"Huh." Emotion builds in my chest and I take a deep breath to calm myself.

"You okay?"

I clear my throat. "Yeah." I squeeze his hand. "Thank you."

"You should talk to her. I can sense the tension when you're together."

I sigh. "I know. It's just . . . hard."

He pulls me into a hug and doesn't say anything else.

I take a few deep breaths and pull away. "Are you really going to surf today? Is your foot better?" I ask, hoping to change the subject. I start walking and take another bite of my apple. I forgot I still had it.

"Good as new." He glances in my direction. "Sleep well last night?"

I swallow and blush. "I could have used a little more."

He chuckles. "I figured since I have to work most of the week, I'd take you out this morning. Sorry I didn't mention it last night. I was a little wired."

"Apparently so was I, since I knocked on your sister's window at two in the morning. Why were you still awake anyway?" I stop walking and throw my apple core in a garbage can.

"Um . . . I wasn't. She came in and woke me up."

"What? Oh my gosh, I'm so sorry! When I saw the light, I thought it was your room. I didn't mean to wake you. If I would have known it was her room in the first place, I wouldn't have even bothered. Can you tell her—"

He puts a finger to my lips and leans in close. "I'm glad you came. Don't be sorry at all."

"But—"

He silences me with a kiss. My toes curl into the sand and when he pulls away, all I can do is stare. I've never kissed anyone in public before. I glance around but no one's even paying attention to us. I look back at him and he searches my face.

"Was that okay? I have to ask. I don't want to move too fast or anything."

Was it okay? Was he kidding?

"Yes!" I blurt and then shut my mouth just as fast. I step back as he starts laughing and we continue toward the beach. We reach the water and walk in until we're about waist deep. "You ready for this?"

"Sure." I gulp and my grip tightens on my board.

"Just stay with me." He plops down on his board and starts paddling out toward the monster waves. I follow suit and he waits patiently for me while I try and keep up.

While he dives into a wave and appears on the other side, I have to push off the bottom and go over it. When we get to deeper water, I struggle to move past the big waves.

I finally reach a calm part of the water and he's waiting for me. He's sitting on his board, his legs dangling in the water. I pull myself into a sitting position and take a few deep breaths. I'm exhausted already. Just from pushing past the waves. "How do you dive in the waves like that? It looks a lot easier than trying not to get smashed by them."

"It's called a duck dive. I'll show you when we come back out." He reaches out and pulls my board closer to his. "Okay. I know you can stand up by yourself in the smaller waves, so these waves won't be too bad. They're not too big today. So, when you see a wave coming, paddle as hard as you can along with it. Then push yourself up and put your arms wide. Like I taught you before."

"That can't be too hard, right?"

He smiles. "And remember to stick your butt out."

"Excuse me?"

"It helps with the balance. Stick your butt out instead of standing straight up." He grins. "Don't worry. I won't be staring too much."

I splash water at him and he laughs.

He looks behind him and turns around with a smile on his face. "Okay. Here comes a good one. Remember to use your core." He touches my stomach and I shiver. "Arms out, balance, and remember that butt."

I'm suddenly really nervous. I feel him push my board forward and start paddling as hard as I can. My adrenaline kicks in as the roar of the wave rushes behind me. I can do this. I can do it. I feel like gravity is working against me as I grab the sides of the board and attempt to stand.

The wave pushes me along as I push up from my knees. My feet touch the board and I'm standing. My arms are wide and I stick my butt out to keep my balance.

"Woo hoo!" I yell, and of course I lose my balance. My face hits the icy water and I'm pretty sure I've been thrown in a washing machine. This time I keep my wits about me and I'm able to find the surface. I can even stand since I've ridden the wave pretty far in. I look out to see if Carson followed me and I spot him riding a wave. He's so smooth and confident in the water. Perfection. He maneuvers his board up and down on the wall of foaming water and finally rides the rest of the way in. He jumps off his board once he's in shallow water and runs to me, splashing water everywhere.

"You did it!" He picks me up and seeing how I'm still hooked to my board and he's still hooked to his, we lose our balance and crash into the water.

I'm laughing so hard I can't breathe. He helps me up and wraps me in a hug. I can't remember the last time I've felt so carefree. It's an amazing feeling. I don't want to lose it.

He pulls away, but only a little. Our hips are pressed against each other and I run my fingers across his chest, feeling his muscles through his wet suit.

He runs his fingers through my wet hair and kisses the tip of my nose. "You ready to go again?"

His gaze is playful, though relaxed. I don't even hesitate when I answer. "Yes! I'll race ya!" He lets me go and I push him out of the way, grab my board, and take off.

"Hey! You cheater! Get back here!"

We spend most of the day on the beach. When I've decided I can't handle the cold water anymore, we head to Carson's house for a bit. As we walk, Carson slips his fingers through my own.

I'm nervous to meet Carson's family. I guess I've already sort of met Keilani but I haven't met either of his parents.

When we reach his house, Carson takes my board and sets it by the front door. He reaches out a hand again and I take it. "You ready?" he asks.

"I guess."

He smiles. "Don't worry. They'll love you." He opens the door and we go inside.

Their house is a lot like Jo's, only with more color. The first thing I notice are all the surfing decorations. They're everywhere. A full-size surfboard hangs across the mantle and there are mini ones situated around the room.

"This must be Oakley," a woman's voice says.

I look up and see a tall, skinny woman coming down the stairs. She's beautiful. I'm guessing she's Polynesian, like I think Keilani is. Her hair is almost to her waist and I can't stop staring at her eyes. Gorgeous brown with super long lashes. She reaches us and holds out a hand. "It's so nice to meet you."

"You as well," I say and shake her hand.

"This is my mom," Carson says.

"Leila," she says with a smile. "And I've heard you've met Keilani."

By the way she's looking at me, she knows I was at her house last night. "I—"

She holds up a hand. "I won't ask any questions. I trust my son."

I can't look at Carson. I'm mortified as it is.

"What's for lunch?" Carson asks. I'm so glad he breaks the silence because I'm ready to run home as fast as I can if his mom says something else.

"Lani's making sandwiches. I'm sure you can talk her into making some for you two." She smiles at me. "It was very good to meet you, Oakley. Take good care of him, won't you? He's a good boy."

"Mom . . ." Carson says, embarrassed.

She starts back up the stairs.

"Is Dad working?" Carson asks.

"Where else would he be?" she says.

Carson mutters something under his breath. I'm curious what he said but don't ask.

We reach the kitchen and Lani already has four turkey sandwiches made. "Hey, guys!" She picks up an empty plate and hands it to Carson. "Hungry? I was just making an after-school snack when I saw you guys through the window. So, being the best sister ever, I made you some too."

"Thanks, Lani. I'm starving." He offers a plate to me and we both grab a sandwich.

We eat in friendly conversation. When I'm done, I turn my attention to Lani. "So . . . Lani," I say. I'm not sure if I'm allowed to call her that but she doesn't seem to mind. "I've heard you're a really good surfer."

She laughs. "I wouldn't say that."

"More like amazing?" Carson says.

She shrugs. "I had a good teacher." She smiles at Carson, who puts a hand on her shoulder.

"You're right about that," he says.

"I'm sure you'll catch up to me in no time," she says to me. "With Carson as your teacher."

"I doubt that," I say.

Carson smiles. "Challenge accepted."

We stay for a few more hours until I'm ready to go. As Carson walks me back to Jo's house, I think about what it will be like back in Utah when spring is over and we go home. I'm not sure how I feel about leaving. There's so much going on that could keep me here. But how could I talk Mom into staying? Does she like it here as much as I do?

"Thanks for coming with me today."

I squeeze Carson's hand. I'm getting used to holding it, even though it's only been for a day—and, thinking back, a few shorter moments here and there. "Thanks for teaching me how to surf again. And for lunch. And for letting me hang out with you and Lani all day."

"It was fun." He swings our hands back and forth before bringing them up and kissing mine. "I was going to ask you . . . what are you doing on Wednesday?"

I shrug. "Nothing, I don't think. Why?"

"I was just making sure you don't have plans with someone else. I'd like to take you out again."

I laugh. "Who would I have plans with?"

"Your mom or Jo?"

"No. No plans."

"Well, I'll make some for us. I work all day tomorrow, but plan on Wednesday, okay?"

"Okay."

"Well, I'll see you then. And I hope you're okay with all this," he says. He gestures to me and himself.

I don't know what to do so I just smile. "I'm more than okay." I'm guessing that was his version of "what are we" talk. Short and sweet. Works for me.

"Good." He leans in and kisses me, his lips as soft as ever. "Goodnight, Oakley."

"Goodnight."

After I shut the door behind me, I hear Jo laughing. "I thought you didn't like him like that?"

I turn around, super embarrassed, but I manage a glare. "Oh, shut up."

She laughs. "Told ya he was a good one."

CHAPTER 17

DEAR OAKLEY,

THERE WAS A TIME IN MY LIFE WHEN I THOUGHT I HAD IT ALL. CAPTAIN OF THE BASKETBALL TEAM, A HOT GIRLFRIEND, STRAIGHT A'S, AND HOPEFULLY A SCHOLARSHIP TO ONE OF MY TOP CHOICE SCHOOLS.

ALL THAT CHANGED WHEN I FOUND OUT I HAD CANCER. I DON'T CARE ABOUT ANY OF THOSE THINGS ANYMORE. I MEAN, I STILL LOVE BASKETBALL, BUT KNOWING I'LL NEVER GET TO PLAY IN COLLEGE HAS MADE ME RETHINK THINGS. ALL THOSE THINGS THAT WERE SO IMPORTANT JUST AREN'T ANYMORE.

I KNOW YOU NEVER LIKED SHELBY. I DON'T REALLY KNOW IF I EVEN LIKED HER. WE WERE JUST SUPPOSED TO DATE. YOU KNOW THE STEREOTYPE. BASKETBALL CAPTAIN, HEAD CHEERLEADER. EVERYONE EXPECTED US TO BE TOGETHER, SO WE WERE. I KNOW SHE LIKED ME, AND I FEEL BAD ABOUT HOW THINGS ENDED, BUT I COULDN'T DO IT ANYMORE. I SHOULD HAVE BROKEN UP WITH HER A LONG TIME AGO. I'M MAD AT MYSELF THAT I DATED HER FOR SO LONG WHEN I WAS IN LOVE WITH SOMEONE ELSE.

EMMY WAS HERE A FEW MINUTES AGO. I FINALLY TOLD HER HOW I FELT. SHE CRIED. I CRIED. I FEEL LIKE A LOSER RIGHT NOW. I SHOULD HAVE TOLD HER YEARS AGO. SHE SHOULD HAVE BEEN MY FIRST KISS SINCE SHE WAS MY FIRST LOVE. BUT SHE SLIPPED AWAY FROM ME A LONG TIME AGO, BECAUSE I WAS TOO CHICKEN TO DO ANYTHING ABOUT IT. AND NOW THAT I KNOW SHE'S IN LOVE WITH ME, TOO, IT BREAKS MY HEART. WE'LL NEVER BE TOGETHER. I'LL NEVER TAKE HER ON A REAL DATE. WE'LL NEVER GET TO GO TO DINNER OR HOLD HANDS OR SIMPLY TALK ABOUT LIFE.

OAKLEY, IF YOU EVER LOVE SOMEONE, DON'T KEEP IT TO YOURSELF. TELL THEM HOW YOU FEEL, EVEN IF YOU DON'T THINK IT WILL WORK OUT. AT LEAST YOU DID IT. AT LEAST YOU TRIED. YOU'LL NEVER KNOW HOW THAT PERSON FEELS ABOUT YOU UNLESS YOU TAKE A CHANCE.

I DID. AND EVEN THOUGH IT'S TOO LATE TO DO ANYTHING ABOUT IT, I'M GLAD I TOOK THAT CHANCE.

LOVE, LUCAS

Poor Emmy. I should call her and see how she's doing, but as always, something stops me. I abandoned my friends. She probably wouldn't even pick up if I did call. She didn't say a word to me at the funeral but I didn't try to talk to anyone, either. It was too painful. And now I realize it was just as painful for her.

I think about Lucas's words. Do I love Carson? No. I can't love someone that soon. Love happens over time.

Months. Years. It's only been a few weeks. It's not possible to feel that much for one person that quickly.

But I can't stop thinking about him. I miss him when he's not around. He makes me happy. He makes me feel whole again. Maybe it's because I crave conversation, or someone's touch. I hate being alone, so maybe the only reason I think about him is because he actually pays attention to me. I shake my head. No. I know I like him but it feels like I'm betraying Lucas's memory by liking him. Not for the first time, I feel like I shouldn't be moving on so quickly.

Jo calls me for breakfast and leaves for work as soon as I meet her in the kitchen. Mom hasn't gotten up yet and I don't plan on waking her. I glance at the clock as I eat my toast. It's almost eight. Carson has already been at work for two hours. Maybe I'll go visit him.

An hour later, I'm riding Jo's bike down the boardwalk. Her bike is old. No, let me rephrase that: it's ancient. But it works and it's the right size. I don't even run anyone or anything over, which makes me more confident.

I reach the surf shop quickly and hop off the bike. I'm not sure where to park, since there are shops and people all around, so I lean it against the store and hope no one steals it. Though if it did end up getting stolen, it would probably give Jo an excuse to buy a nicer bike.

Keilani is at the desk when I walk in. She's waxing a surfboard and glances up as the little bell rings above me. She smiles wide when she sees me.

"Hey," I say. "Is Carson working?"

"He's in the back. Come with me," she says.

She leads me to the back of the store and through a door. She shuts it behind her and gestures to the left. Piles of surfboards are stacked against the walls on either side of the hallway and Carson's holding a clipboard near the end of it.

"Hey," he says. His face brightens and he walks over and pulls me into a hug. "What are you doing here?"

"I just thought I'd stop by and see how you're doing."

"I'm glad you did. Inventory is seriously killing me." He sets down his clipboard and lets out an exasperated sigh. "You look cute today."

I tuck my hair behind my ear, feeling flustered. "Oh. Thanks." My mind is jumbled but I manage to talk again. "I know you have to get back to work but I brought you a treat. If you want it."

"Really?" His eyes widen. "What is it?"

I pull a package of cinnamon almonds out of my purse. "I don't know if you like these, but—"

"I love them!" He takes the package with a sort of reverence. "Thank you so much."

A voice booms right outside the door, making me jump. He glances toward the door and frowns. "I'd better get back to work. My dad wants this done today so I have to hurry or I'll be here all night."

"Okay. I'll see you later. Or talk to you later. Or . . . something."

He chuckles. "You're cute when you're nervous."

"I'm not nervous."

"Whatever you say." He smiles and leans down to give me a quick kiss.

"Ew. Gross. You kissed my brother," Keilani says.

"Sorry," I say, blushing.

She nudges my shoulder and smiles. "Come on. I'll walk you outside so Carson doesn't get in trouble for bringing his personal life to work."

My eyes widen. "Would he really get in trouble?"

She just laughs and shakes her head.

She goes through the door and I follow. As soon as it shuts, I come face to face with an older, taller Carson. I know it's his dad. He seriously looks just like him—besides the gray running through his light brown hair and the wrinkles around his eyes. "Well, who do we have here?" He looks down at me, a serious, focused expression on his face.

"Um . . . I'm Oakley."

"Oh. Right. The neighbor girl. You're the one who's spending all the time with my son."

I'm so scared I could pee my pants right now and not even care.

"I'm . . . sorry?" I don't know why I make it a question. I just want him to stop staring at me like I'm a piece of gum stuck to the bottom of his shoe.

He's still looking at me so I give him a small smile. "Um . . . it was nice to meet you." I hurry through the store and out the already open door. Once I'm outside, I take a few breaths and try to compose myself. After a moment, I hear raised voices coming from inside.

186

"Did you really have to treat her like that?" Carson says, sounding angrier than I've ever heard him.

"You know the rules, Carson. We have a reputation. Do you think I made the rules to have my own son break them?"

"Dad, he didn't invite her to come hang out here all day, she just came to say hi. It's not like she made him stop working or anything. It's not a big deal," Lani says.

"It is a big deal. She's a distraction. A big one, I've noticed. I know she's been screwing with your head, Carson, and I don't like it. I don't know anything about her, and frankly, neither do you."

"Dad—"

"The point is, when you're at this store, you work. You don't invite your little girlfriends over to play. And if you're going to take over my shop someday, I need you to focus."

"You know I don't want to take over the shop, Dad."

"We're not going to talk about this right now."

"Why not? Every time we try to, you say the same thing. Not right now. What's wrong with right now?"

He's quiet for a moment and I lean a little closer to the door. I shouldn't be eavesdropping but I can't help it.

His dad speaks again, quieter this time. "I just don't understand it. I don't understand why you don't want to do this forever. You're a natural surfer, you sell more than half the surfboards in here. People know your name. You could be famous. I know you're good enough to win some of those competitions. Don't you want that? You could get sponsored and make a wonderful living surfing and making and selling surfboards. Why would you want to give that all up to spend thousands of dollars on a degree you might not even use?"

It's quiet.

"You're right," Carson says. "You don't understand. I have my own dreams, Dad. And they're not the same as yours. With the degree *I* want, I can do what I love."

It's quiet for a moment. I don't dare move.

"You were set in your ways until you met that girl."

"Her name's Oakley. And I've been thinking about what I want to do with my life way before I met her."

"I don't want to see her here with you again. Do you understand?"

"Dad, come on," Lani says, still trying to help the situation.

"Get back to work, Lani."

I hear a door slam in the background. Carson, maybe? I move to get on my bike, to get out of here before anything else can go wrong, just as Lani comes outside. By the surprised look on her face, she knows I've heard every word.

"Oakley, wait," she says, but I ride home as fast as I can and don't look back.

I sit on the beach by myself for a long time. The tide is coming in but I don't care. I need to be alone and think.

I like Carson. A lot. I really do. And now that I know his dad hates me, I'm not sure what my next move should be. What am I going to do? Should I talk to Carson about it? I don't want to turn him against his dad. That would be horrible.

Footsteps interrupt my thoughts and I look up to see Dillon standing in front of me.

"Hey." He doesn't ask, just sits next to me and stares out into the water.

"Hi." He always shows up at the most random times. I still don't know what to think of him and I wonder where he lives that he always seems to be nearby.

He shifts next to me. "Look, I know it's none of my business but I have to say it. Carson's a good guy, Oakley. And when he falls for someone, he falls hard. I don't want him to get hurt."

"What?"

"I've talked to Jo a few times. I know you're leaving at the end of the spring. Carson really likes you. Like, *really* likes you. And if you keep leading him on the way you are, you'll break him when you leave."

I'll break him? Does Dillon have any idea what it will do to *me*? I don't lead people on. If Dillon thinks I'm playing a game with Carson, he's wrong.

"Do you think I'm just looking for a fling or something? Because I can assure you, that's not what this is."

He turns to look at me. "Then what is it?"

I open my mouth, then close it. I can't answer him. I honestly have no idea what Carson and I are doing.

He smiles. "I thought so." He sits there for a minute or so before he speaks again. "Let him down easy, okay?" He stands and wipes the sand from his shorts. "I'll see you later."

I stare after him as he walks away. My whole body is shaking. Why does Dillon care so much? He doesn't seem like the type who would care about his friend's feelings, as crappy as that sounds.

The more I sit there, though, the more I realize he's right. I *am* leaving. I don't want to hurt him. And what does he even see in me anyway? I have so much emotional baggage that could explode at any second and he can still stand to be around me? *I* don't even like to be around me.

Dillon's right. We shouldn't be together because I bring him down. I know Lucas said I should share my feelings when I like someone, but I can't. Lucas didn't get the chance until it was too late and look where that got him. If I don't say anything to Carson about how much I've come to like him, my feelings will eventually go away. It will be like we never even met. He'll forget about me soon enough. After all, there are plenty of other girls around here who would love to have him.

I close my eyes. I don't want to hurt him. He's so . . . good. But if I really feel the way I think I feel about him, then I have to let him go. I can't keep stringing him along when I know I'm going to leave him. It wouldn't be fair to either one of us. And I've heard horror stories of long-distance relationships. Most of them don't last. Better to break it off now in person than through a text message from another state.

I walk back to Jo's house, ignoring her concerned look when I come through the door. I head straight for my room, lie down on my bed, and sob in the darkness.

CHAPTER 18

DEAR OAKLEY,

REMEMBER THAT BOX OF CRAP I USED TO HAVE HIDDEN IN MY CLOSET AS A KID? AND NO, DON'T TAKE THAT LITERALLY. LIKE COOL ROCKS AND MARBLES AND STUFF. I STILL HAVE IT. MY OLD COWBOY HAT IS IN THERE, TOO. I CAN SEE YOU FROWNING RIGHT NOW. I KNOW HOW MUCH YOU PRETEND TO HATE MY HATS, BUT YOU KNOW THEY RULE.

I'LL PAY YOU FIVE BUCKS IF YOU WEAR IT AROUND FOR ONE DAY. THERE'S FIVE BUCKS IN MY BOTTOM DRAWER, TAPED TO THE BACK OF IT. IT'S YOURS. BUT ONLY IF YOU WEAR THE HAT.

I TRIPLE DOG DARE YOU.

LOVE, LUCAS

There is no way I'll ever wear that hat.

I didn't see Carson yesterday but he texted me late last night and told me he'd pick me up Wednesday morning.

I'm still in a bad mood from both of my not–so–awesome encounters yesterday with Carson's dad and Dillon.

I decide on shorts and a red tank. My red flip-flops match perfectly and I keep my hair down. I haven't worn it that way in a while.

Carson picks me up early and, to my surprise, has something in his hands I'd never thought I'd ever use again.

"Rollerblades?"

His grin is huge as he hands me a pair with pink laces. "Aren't they awesome? I thought we'd start the morning off right."

"Is Rollerblading really that big a thing around here? Because I haven't worn those for like ten years." I finger the pink laces and smile at all my Rollerblading memories from childhood.

"Haven't you seen people wearing them on the boardwalk? I see a few a day at least." He glances at my blades. "Hopefully they're the right size. I kind of guessed."

I peek at the tag inside of one. It's an eight. I'm a seven and a half. "Close enough."

"Great. Let's get going then." He has two helmets in his hand and grins when he sees me looking at them. "Safety first," he says, winking.

I thought biking with Carson a few weeks ago was hard but it's nothing compared to Rollerblading. Once I get the skates on, I can barely balance enough to stay on my feet. I know it's been a while since I've done this, but this is ridiculous. I hang onto a palm tree near the boardwalk and watch Carson skate around like it's nothing. I swear he's good at everything.

He cracks up at the terrified look on my face and holds out a hand. "You coming or what?"

"I think?" I let go of the tree and roll over to him without even moving my legs. Maybe I'll just have him pull me along. That would be easiest, I think.

"It's just like walking."

"I know. It's just been a long time." It takes me a few minutes but once I have the hang of it, I'm gliding next to Carson without using him for support.

"See? I knew you could do it."

"It's coming back to me!" I glance over at him. "Race ya!"

"You're on." We book it down the boardwalk even though I'm still being a little cautious. Oh, how I wish Lucas were here. He loved these things even more than I did when we were little.

Carson passes me, then slows down for me to catch up and I laugh. "I forgot how fun this is!" I pick up speed, weaving around a few people jogging on the boardwalk. Carson stays either right beside me or behind and I can't keep the smile off my face the entire time. I'm glad we did this today. It will be a good memory of the last time we'll be together before I go back to Utah.

"We'll stop at the boardwalk if that's okay."

"Sounds great."

We've been blading for a while now and my legs and lower back are starting to ache. Hopefully I'll be able to make it back to home later. Once we near the pier,

I realize something. "Um . . . Carson? How am I supposed to stop?"

"Just slow down and you'll eventually roll to a stop. Or you can turn in kind of a circle and stop, but maybe we should just stick with you slowing down for now. . ." He trails off and grins.

But I can't slow down. We're kind of in a hilly area. Not really a noticeable hill, but I'm definitely going faster rather than slower. Before I know it, my arms are flailing and I'm headed toward a garbage can on the pier.

"Hold on!" Carson shouts and before I can react, he reaches out and grabs my hand. I jerk around in almost a complete circle and slam into his chest. I don't know how he doesn't fall over but somehow he holds us both up as we laugh our heads off.

"Dumpster diving in the morning? Don't you have anything better to do?"

I giggle and push him away, rolling backward into the garbage can, which sends us both into another fit of laughter.

Once I gain my balance again, I plop down on some grass near the trail. "So, are we Rollerblading on the pier? Is that allowed?"

"Not exactly. Just a second." He glances past me and waves. I turn around and see Keilani heading toward us, a plastic bag in her hand.

I look back at Carson, who's grinning. "What is this?"

"I told you I wanted to spend the day with you, so I came prepared."

"Hey, you two," Keilani says. "That was some wild Rollerblading work, Oakley. I was sort of hoping you would take a dive into that garbage can."

"Yeah, I'm pretty sure Carson was too." I glance at him and he just shrugs.

"So, here's the stuff you asked for." She hands Carson the bag. "You owe me."

"I know."

"I'm glad we understand each other." She grins. "Everything else is underway. Hand over the blades and I'll take them back to the shop for you."

Carson takes his Rollerblades off and hands them to her, and after a moment's hesitation, I do the same.

Once Keilani has the Rollerblades, she backs up. "I'll see you two later." She winks and leaves us alone.

I watch her walk away as Carson fishes through the bag. "Here you go." He hands me my red flip-flops.

"Where did you get these?"

"I told Jo that Keilani would be over to get them after we left. I didn't want to carry the bag while we were rollerblading in case you . . . wiped out or something."

I nod. Makes sense.

"You ready?"

"Yep."

He helps me up. "Time to get acquainted with Huntington Beach."

The day goes by slow at first. I'm grateful for every moment I spend with him, so it's a good thing. Carson shows me around everywhere. And I mean *everywhere*.

A surfing museum, historic sites around the pier that I know I won't remember the names of . . . but it's okay. As long as I'm with him, nothing else seems to matter.

Carson holds my hand wherever we go and I'm happy, but I still can't get the words Dillon said out of my head. I don't want to hurt Carson. And Dillon's right. I will hurt him when I leave next month. Or the month after that. Whenever Mom's ready, I guess. The point is, I need to focus on getting over Lucas's death. That's the whole reason I came here. He'd be disappointed in me for putting all my efforts into a relationship when I'm supposed to be getting myself together.

The rest of the day goes by in a blur. We finally eat at Ruby's for dinner, which is yummy and awesome because it's surrounded by water around the pier. Once we finish, though, there are so many people around the shops and pier that I start to feel a little claustrophobic. Carson takes me home so I can change my clothes into something more comfortable since he said I might get chilly wherever we're going next. Once I'm freshened up, Carson takes me across the street to the beach.

It's still pretty light outside and I watch the tide slowly come in as the sun starts to go down, and as usual, I slip my shoes off to walk in the shallow water. Carson leads me down the beach until we reach the spot where I first met him. Close to the tide pools.

There's a blanket already set up on the sand with a picnic basket sitting in the middle of it. I glance around.

Obviously someone was just here. I'm guessing Keilani had something to do with it.

"You like it?" Carson asks as we sit down.

"Like it?" I glance at him, trying not to cry. "I love it. Thank you."

He shrugs and I see a slight blush hit his cheeks. "I just wanted to do something nice instead of making you surf or Rollerblade or do stuff you don't really care to do."

"You haven't made me do anything I didn't want to do."

"Good. Sorry if your legs are sore. My ankles are killing me actually."

"Mine too, but it was worth it."

He smiles and leans back on his hands, his legs stretched out in front of him. "The sunset is nice tonight."

"It is."

We're sitting close but not super close, and as much as I want to cuddle with him, something's stopping me.

Stupid Dillon.

"You've been really quiet today. Everything okay?"

I turn to look at him and nod. "Yep."

He stares at me for a second before sitting up. "You're sure?"

I nod. I'm not about to go into it. He's been so sweet today. And not just today. I sigh. I don't know what to do.

Carson reaches for the picnic basket. "I thought we could eat a little dessert and then I invited some company to play games."

"Sounds great." I wonder who he invited.

He pulls out two pieces of cheesecake and I'm sure my eyes are huge as I watch him set it on a small plate in front of me. I hope I'm not drooling.

"You like cheesecake?"

"Um . . . yes. My favorite."

"Great!"

I'm not afraid to finish my piece, even though it's enormous. As soon as I pop the last delicious bite in my mouth, I hear a shout from behind.

"Hey, guys!"

I turn around to see Keilani and Dillon walking toward us. Dillon sits down right next to me and Lani sits on his other side. "Bring on the games," he says. He gives me a strange look and I glance away.

"Thanks for bringing that basket down, Lani." Carson says.

"Of course. I told you, you'd owe me." Lani laughs. "Nothing like your little sister tagging along, right?"

"Best company ever," Carson says. He nudges my shoulder. "Besides you, of course."

I give him a small smile. I'm not sure about the company now that Dillon's here.

We settle into a few games of Phase 10. The worst game ever. I call it Phase Hour 10 because it goes on for-freaking-ever. I suck at card games so it isn't a surprise when I lose.

"Good game, Oakley." Dillon smiles and nudges my shoulder.

"Thanks. I'm a natural."

Carson laughs. "You've really never won a single game?"

I shake my head. "Nope. I told you, I suck."

"I'm sure you'll get better if you play more often."

"Not likely."

He laughs.

After talking for a while, or I guess listening to Lani and Dillon talk, argue, and talk some more, Lani yawns and stands. "I'd better get home. I have school tomorrow." She holds out a hand to Dillon, who looks reluctant to take it. "And you have work, I believe."

She shoots him a look and he sighs before taking her hand. "Yeah, I do."

"Have a good night you two," she calls before slipping her arm through his and walking away. Dillon looks back a few times, his eyes meeting mine before he turns around for good. I know what he's trying to tell me.

I need to let Carson know it's over now. But how can I do that when it's been one of the best days of my life? I glance up at the stars, wondering if Lucas will help me be strong and my breath catches. The stars are beautiful tonight. Brighter than I remember.

"The stars look awesome on the water tonight," Carson says. He scoots close, wraps an arm around my shoulder, and kisses my temple. I don't scoot away, just enjoy these last few moments with him.

"Yeah." It's all I can say without losing it.

I can't do it anymore. I have to let him go before I get too attached. Because I'm attached already and it's not like we've even been together that long. Which might make things much easier. Maybe it won't hurt as much.

We sit in silence for a while, listening to the waves crash onto the beach. I tell myself to remember this moment. The way Carson's arm feels around my shoulders. The smell of the salty air, the beautiful bright stars glistening over the water. I don't realize I'm crying until Carson says something.

"What?" I ask. A tear slides down my cheek and I wipe it away quickly.

"Are you okay?" He reaches out and wipes another tear with his finger.

I shake my head. "No. I'm not." I pull away and stand. "Thank you, for . . . all this. For everything. But I've got to go now. I'm sorry."

I leave him sitting there and start down the beach, hoping he'll take the hint not to follow.

"Oakley, wait!" I hear his feet in the sand as he catches up and I cringe. I don't want to do this but I have to. I have to let him go. "What's wrong? What did I do?"

"Nothing," I say, stopping to look at him. "You haven't done anything. That's the problem." *You're perfect and I don't want to hurt you, but we can't be together. I'll just end up leaving and never see you again.*

He reaches out to me but I step back. "At least let me walk you home."

"I can walk home myself."

He frowns. "Something's up, Oakley. Talk to me. What's wrong and how can I fix it?"

"There's nothing to fix. I'm just . . . sorry I got too close. I'm sorry about everything." I turn to leave again but he grabs my hand, soft and gentle, but enough to pull me to a stop.

"Oakley, wait," he says, pulling me closer. "Please. Talk to me."

"There's nothing else to say."

He stares at me a moment before dropping my hand. "Right. Nothing else to say." He takes a deep breath and runs a hand through his hair. He looks agitated. Even a little angry. "Do you do this to everyone who cares about you? Push them away? Or am I just lucky?"

"I don't push people away."

"Really." He folds his arms and frowns. "For some reason it's hard to believe you. What about your mom?"

"What about her?"

"Ever since you came here I've seen you talk to her maybe once. I see the way you avoid each other. Just like you're trying to avoid me now."

"I'm not trying to avoid you."

He sighs and reaches for my hand. "Help me understand what the problem is then. I care about you, Oakley. And I thought you cared enough about me to talk to me about things. I thought we . . . today was . . . awesome. Wasn't it?"

"It was." I try to shake off the emotion that creeps in. "And I do care about you. That's the problem."

"You caring about me is the problem?" He raises his voice and glances around before stepping closer. "If you care about me so much, then why are you walking away from me right now?"

I meet his gaze and want to tell him exactly how I feel. How he's wonderful and amazing and makes me feel alive—something I haven't felt since before Lucas died. But I can't do it. I'm a coward, too afraid to fall in love and be happy, too afraid of possibly losing someone else I love.

"I'm sorry." I gesture to myself and then to him. "I can't do this anymore."

"Can't do what? Our relationship? Help me out here, Oakley, because obviously I've done something to piss you off enough to break up with me."

"You haven't done anything." I shake my head, tears fill my eyes. "I'm just . . . sorry." I turn around, take off running, and don't look back.

CHAPTER 19

DEAR OAKLEY,

EVERYONE WAS SO SAD WHEN THEY VISITED ME TODAY. I KNOW IT'S MY FAULT. EVER SINCE I GOT SICK IT HAS BEEN A BURDEN ON EVERYONE. AND I'M SORRY FOR THAT. I WISH I COULD MAKE YOU GUYS HAPPY AGAIN.

OUR FAMILY WAS NEVER SUPER CLOSE, BUT WE'VE ALWAYS GOTTEN ALONG. DON'T LOSE THAT, OAKLEY. DON'T LET OUR FAMILY BREAK APART. DON'T LET MOM WASTE AWAY WITHOUT SMILING. MAKE HER SMILE AGAIN. SHE DESERVES TO BE HAPPY. AND SO DO YOU.

LOVE, LUCAS

I miss the days of laughing and smiling. Right when I thought I was getting better, everything falls to crap.

Carson's called my cell three times and the house twice. I refuse to answer. Mom has asked me what's wrong but I won't talk to her. I can't. I feel horrible. Carson deserves an explanation but I don't dare face him.

I need time to sort out my jumbled thoughts. I need time to figure out what I want and who I really am. My life is spiraling down, and honestly, Carson is the only one who even attempted to pull me back up.

It's only been a day and I miss him. I wonder if he's calling because he's angry or if he wants to see me. Maybe he misses me too.

The sun beats down on me as I sit on the front porch steps, doing nothing, saying nothing. Just staring at the ocean across the street, wondering if Carson's surfing today and wishing I was brave enough to figure myself out.

The door opens behind me and Jo steps outside. I know it's her since Mom is gone today. Again. "Hey. Mind if I join ya?"

I shrug. "Sure."

She sits next to me, her fingers playing with the tangles in her wild hair. "You've been moping around here all day. If something's bothering you, it helps to talk about it."

I let out a slow breath and keep my eyes focused on the bits of sand scattered on her sidewalk. "Only if you have something to talk about." I don't want to talk about Carson and pray she doesn't bring him up.

"Fair enough." She pulls something onto her lap and I glance at it. A scrapbook or something?

"What is that?"

She smiles. "I was hoping you'd like to look at it with me." She flips the page open and I'm suddenly staring into a two-year-old Lucas's face.

"What . . . where did you get that?" I lean closer, taking in his toothy grin and platinum blond hair.

"I have a lot more." She sets half of the book on my lap and flips the page.

There are dozens of pictures of Lucas and me. From when we were babies, all the way up to the present. I stare at us when we were twelve and fourteen. His freckled face with a huge grin and me standing next to him, my hair shorter and lighter, laughing at something he probably said. "Where did you get all these?"

She shrugs. "Your mom."

"She sent them to you?"

"Hun, you're my only family. Did you think since I lived so far away I wouldn't have pictures of my favorite niece and nephew?"

I touch the freckled Lucas again. "I never thought about it."

She's quiet for a moment. "He always took good care of you, didn't he." It's not a question but I swallow the lump in my throat and nod anyway.

"Yes," I whisper.

My fingers flip through some of the last pages. The ones taken a year or so ago. There's one of me holding up a medal from a swim meet. That one I remember Lucas took. One of Lucas playing basketball that I remember taking. There's one of Lucas laughing and holding on to the strings of my hoodie, my nose the only part of me showing since he had pulled my hood so tight.

I stare at the last picture for a long time. It's of Lucas in his hospital bed giving a thumbs up with one hand and covering my laughing face with his other.

"Thank you. For sharing this with me." My shaky voice can't hide the depth of my sorrow but somehow I manage to keep it together.

"You're welcome. And you know I'll always be here to talk if you need me. I know a thing or two about boys, you know."

I crack a smile. "Thanks." I'm grateful she doesn't press me for details. It's obvious she knows I'm avoiding Carson but she hasn't brought it up, even when I've told her to tell him I'm not available when he calls.

She's wonderful. My aunt.

Jo wraps her arm around my shoulders and gives me a squeeze before letting go. "I love ya, kid. So do your parents. Especially your mom. She may not show it all the time, or in the way you need, but she does. You're all she has left."

"I know."

CHAPTER 20

DEAR OAKLEY,

TODAY WAS A ROTTEN DAY. THE XBOX GAMES YOU BROUGHT ME PUT ME IN A BETTER MOOD, SO THANKS FOR THAT. NOTHING LIKE KILLING A BUNCH OF ALIENS TO PASS THE TIME. YOU ALWAYS KNOW HOW TO CHEER ME UP.

I MISS YOU WHEN YOU GO HOME FOR THE NIGHT. I'LL NEVER TELL YOU THAT TO YOUR FACE, SINCE YOU'D STAY AS LONG AS I WANT YOU TO, BUT IT'S TRUE. I MISS YOU WHEN YOU LEAVE. YOU'RE THE ONE I'M FIGHTING FOR. THE ONLY ONE WHO'S BEEN WITH ME THROUGH THIS ENTIRE ORDEAL. SO, THANK YOU. THANK YOU FOR BEING MY BEST FRIEND AND LETTING ME KICK YOUR BUTT AT UNO AND PHASE 10 DAY AFTER DAY. AND PRETEND-ING YOU CAN PLAY XBOX, BECAUSE YOU REALLY CAN'T. BUT YOU ALREADY KNOW THAT.

OH, AND BY THE WAY, WHEN I'M GONE? ALL THESE GAMES ARE YOURS. TAKE CARE OF THEM AND DON'T YOU DARE SELL THEM! YOU'RE GONNA HAVE KIDS SOMEDAY AND EVEN THOUGH THE GAMES WILL BE ANCIENT BY THEN, I WANT THEM TO HAVE SOMETHING FROM THEIR UNCLE LUCAS.

NIGHT!

LOVE, LUCAS

It's been a week. I can only stay holed up in my room for so long and I'm starting to go crazy. Jo took me on another one of her jobs, which I was grateful for. This time to save a baby sea lion trapped in some fishing line, but as soon as they got it free and monitored it for a bit, we came back home and I fell into my routine of sitting in my room, playing my guitar for a few minutes, and then staring at my pictures on my wall.

My glamorous and boring life.

I still haven't talked to Carson. He hasn't given up though. He's knocked on my door several times, called, texted me, talked to Jo. I stare at the latest text and sigh.

I need to talk to you. Please call me back.

I turn off my phone. I don't know what else to do.

I've seen him a few times since I left him at the beach. But not up close. I've watched him surf and not wanting to be a stalker but wanting to have a few pictures of him, I took my camera with me and snapped a few. Then I went home and locked myself in my room again.

It's funny how girls can be so dramatic. I always thought girls were stupid in the movies I'd watch. How they'd run away from problems and never talk about it. But I'm acting the same exact way. And it's slowly driving me insane. I know I'm being ridiculous. I know I should explain things to Carson but part of me still believes that I'm not good enough for him. I don't want to give myself false hope that maybe I *am* good enough.

I can't help but think what Lucas would say if he were here. Actually, I know exactly what he'd say.

Don't be stupid, Oakley. Talk to him.

I pick up my phone again and my fingers hover over the keypad. I sigh and set it down again.

Maybe tomorrow.

CHAPTER 21

DEAR OAKLEY,

THEY'RE LETTING ME COME HOME TOMORROW. I KNOW WHAT WILL HAPPEN WHEN I GET THERE. MY BODY HURTS. I'M TIRED. I CAN FEEL THE STRAIN OF ALL THE CHEMICALS AND MEDICINE PUSHING ME INTO A BLACK HOLE. I CAN'T TAKE IT ANYMORE. IF I WERE STRONGER, MAYBE I'D FIGHT HARDER, BUT IT'S A LOST CAUSE.

I'M GLAD I'LL BE HOME WHEN IT HAPPENS. BE WITH YOU AND MOM AND DAD. I'M NOT READY TO LEAVE THIS LIFE JUST YET, BUT I DON'T HAVE A CHOICE. I KNOW I'LL BE OKAY. I'M JUST WORRIED ABOUT YOU. YOU'RE THE REASON I'VE LASTED THIS LONG. YOU KEEP TELLING ME TO STAY STRONG AND FIGHT. BUT I'M DONE FIGHTING. SO I'LL TELL YOU THIS, AND YOU'D BETTER DO IT. STAY STRONG FOR ME.

LOVE, LUCAS

I feel numb. Thinking about Lucas's last days is almost more than I can handle. I close the notebook and sit there, staring at the floor. I've been strong. At least I think I have. What else does he want me to do?

What if things had been different? What if it had been me fighting instead of him? He'd still be alive. He'd still have a chance with Emmy. But either way, we wouldn't be together. He'd lose his sister or I'd lose my brother. Neither is fair.

I look out the window and sigh. I need to talk to someone. I should start with Mom, but the timing has to be right. For both of us. My thoughts turn to Carson. I need to apologize for acting like a freak and I wonder if whatever he felt about me is gone now. The longer I've had to think about it, the more I've realized how stupid I've been. I haven't been following Lucas's advice the way he intended. I haven't been taking risks; I haven't been living. I've been on the cusp but I've let fear of the unknown and of loss hold me back. And now I know—I want to be with Carson. I want to see where it goes, even if I'm going to leave someday. Why can't we see if it can work out until that day comes? And then, maybe even after that.

I have to find him and explain my crazy self to him. I really hope he'll forgive me.

I tell Mom where I'm going and head outside to the beach. I know exactly where to find him, unless he's at work, which I hope he's not.

There aren't many surfers out, which makes me feel a little less scared. I can move easier without having to worry about people running me over. The sky is a light gray and the wind is blowing a little.

Carson's already out there. I recognize his yellow board as he falls off a wave. I'm not sure what I'm going to say to him but I do know we have a lot to talk about. I'll apologize first and go from there.

I grab my board and enter the water. It's colder than I remember, though it might be because I'm not wearing a wet suit. When the water is to my waist, I jump on my board and start paddling. As I break the swell, I'm surprised to see Carson sitting just behind it. He's waiting for me. His usual smile is gone and his dark eyes look sad.

"Hey," I say. I sit up on my board so my legs dangle in the water. It's murkier than usual. I can't see my legs at all.

"Hey," he says. He watches me for a second before looking toward the beach.

"Waves any good today?" Stupid. What a way to start the conversation. I know he's mad at me and now he probably thinks I don't care. I wait for him to answer but he just shrugs.

"Carson," I start.

He holds up a hand. "You don't have to explain anything."

"Yes I do."

"You've been pretty clear about where we stand and I really don't think I can handle hearing any more."

I sigh. "Please. Let me explain. I screwed up, okay?"

He's quiet, staring at the water in front of him.

"Could you please just listen to me for a second? Please?"

"Sure." He still won't look at me but I start talking anyway.

"First of all, I want to say I'm sorry. I had no reason to ignore you the past week. I've never had a boyfriend before. I don't know what to do or how to act. I wasn't sure what I was feeling. Everything was so confusing. It still is." I shake my head. "I'm so sorry I ruined everything."

He turns to look at me and opens his mouth to say something, but I beat him to it.

"I've had a lot of time to think since I've moved here. After Lucas died . . . I never thought I'd get over it. And I'm not over it. But I'm starting to move on. The only reason I've gotten this far is because of you. You've helped me heal. You haven't given up on me and I don't understand why." I wish he could understand how much he's helped me. It's so hard to open up to anybody but for some reason it's easy with him.

"Why did you ignore me?" he asks. "What did I do?"

I lift my eyes to meet his. They're curious, but patient. Always so patient. "It wasn't anything you did . . ." I hesitate. I think about what Dillon said to me. That's the biggest reason. I don't want to be the bad guy. And I'm not, but it might seem like I am if I tell him what he said. And then all the stuff his dad said . . . I take a deep breath. "Dillon said some stuff."

He frowns. "What kind of stuff?"

"He wasn't trying to be mean, he just told me some things. You know I'm leaving before summer starts. He doesn't want me to lead you on and leave you. He doesn't want you to get hurt."

"Are you serious?" He rolls his eyes. "Of course he said that. He likes you."

"What? No he doesn't."

"Look. I've known Dillon for a long time and he's never cared enough about my feelings to tell the girl I like to break up with me because he doesn't want me to get hurt. He's mad that you never gave him the time of day." He shakes his head and studies me. "That's not the only reason you've been ignoring me. What else?"

I run my hand through the water and avoid his eyes. "I have too much baggage."

He shrugs. "So do I."

"Not like mine."

"Everyone has baggage, Oakley. No one's perfect. If you think that's going to scare me off, you're wrong."

"It should."

He reaches across the water and grabs my hand. He's so serious. My body shakes from the cold but he holds on. "It doesn't."

"I feel like I'm betraying Lucas, though. That me being happy will make him sad. I'm supposed to be grieving. And I feel . . . guilty. That I'm getting to experience these amazing things with you that he never got to feel."

He sighs. "You think he'll be sad to know you're living your life and that you're happy? I don't think so. I think he'd be proud of you for moving on. You don't have to forget someone to move on. They can still be with you. And all the memories you had together? They never go away."

"I know they won't go away. But it's still hard knowing I won't have any new memories with him to look forward to."

"I know. I also know he wouldn't want you to be miserable." He squeezes my hand. "What else?"

What else? I don't know what else. I mean, I do, I just don't know if I want to say. I've never been good about sharing my feelings. He's kind of pushing it. I meet his eyes. He's watching me. His expression curious, but soft.

"The truth is . . . I . . . I'm going to miss you when I leave. I don't want to get involved with someone I might not ever see again. I don't want to be just a fling."

He smiles. "Trust me. This isn't a fling. What I feel for you I've never felt for anyone else. You're stubborn and funny. Shy and withdrawn, but when I somehow break those barriers, you're sweet and caring. You're so talented and beautiful. If you'd see yourself like I see you . . ." His voice catches and he shakes his head with a smile. "I've thought about you every single day since the first day I met you. I know they say there's no such thing as love at first sight, but I think they're wrong. I knew I wanted to date you the second you almost fell into that tide pool. It took a little convincing but I finally got you to agree. Somehow."

I don't know what to say. I'm shocked, to say the least. I certainly didn't fall for him that quickly. And even though he didn't say *I love you*, maybe that's what he means. In the tone of his voice and the way he's looking at me. I don't know if I love him back yet, but if I stop being an idiot, maybe I can figure it out.

He squeezes my hand. "You're perfect for me, you know that?"

I blush. "I'm pretty sure *you're* the perfect one."

He searches my face and squeezes my hand again. "And don't talk about leaving yet. We have the rest of the spring and we could have the summer, right?"

"Maybe."

He looks around. We've floated a little ways out. "Let's go in. You're cold. We can talk on the beach while you warm up."

There are a million things I want to say to him, but I just nod instead. We'll have time to talk later. "Okay."

He drops my hand, and as I go to paddle, something hits my board so hard it knocks me into the water. I hear Carson shout my name before I go under.

Something slides past my legs and I panic as I scramble to the surface.

Carson's still yelling and it takes me a second to realize what's happening.

"Shark!" he yells. "Get back to the beach, *now!*"

The danger must be real, or he wouldn't be yelling, but there is no way I'm leaving him out here. I grab my board, climb on as fast as I can, and paddle frantically toward him.

I'm almost to him when I see the monstrous fin slice through the water a few feet away. My stomach drops and I freeze as it heads straight for Carson. I watch in terror as he's knocked off his board and hits the water with a splash. I scream his name as he disappears. He surfaces just as quick, but the second he locks eyes with me, he's dragged under.

I don't think, I just move. I'm screaming Carson's name as I unhook my ankle and leave the safety of my board. The water is red all around me and I start to panic when Carson doesn't surface for what seems like minutes, but it's probably only seconds. I look around, not knowing what to do as screams echo along the beach behind me.

And then Carson's head pops up only a few feet away. The shark still has him and he's fighting to get away. It takes only seconds for me to swim close enough to see the shark's dark eye. I don't think, just punch any part of the fish that I can.

Without warning, the shark releases him, and I grab Carson under the arms. I pull him toward my board. "Carson," I cry over and over, but he doesn't answer. I glance around, terrified the shark will come back, but my only focus now is to get Carson to the beach. I try to keep his head above the water as I kick my legs as hard as I can.

I'm sobbing. I have no idea where my board is and we're surrounded in red. My legs feel like Jell-O and I'm pretty sure I'm going into shock. I get a sliver of hope when Carson says my name but then he passes out again and starts going under. I can't hold him, I'm shaking so bad and, just when I think I'll drown us both, Dillon appears at my side, along with three surfers I've never seen before. They pull Carson away from me and Dillon grabs my arm and steers me toward my board, which is floating a few yards away. I don't know how I didn't see it before.

"Are you hurt?" he yells. I stare at him. I can't feel my body anymore. Everything is numb. "Oakley!" He grabs my face and it takes me a second to focus on him. "Are you hurt?"

"Where's Carson?" I ask. My voice sounds tiny, like a child.

He glances behind us. "There's an ambulance on its way. He's almost to the beach." He looks around. "We've got to get out of the water in case it comes back."

He grabs my board and paddles us into the beach. When we're close enough, he helps me stand. I lean on him for support.

"Your hands," he says.

I look down and notice a few knuckles are bleeding. Did I really punch a shark? The whole thing feels like a dream. That couldn't have been me. I'm not strong enough or brave enough to do something like that.

Keilani meets us in the water and asks me something. She's crying. I don't understand a word she says. All I can hear are sirens.

And people yelling.

I look ahead and see Carson motionless on the ground. His wet suit is ripped to shreds. The sand is turning red underneath him. Paramedics are all around him, pressing and bandaging his wounds. One of them is giving him CPR.

Then I see it: only one foot where there should be two. I take a step forward, just to make sure. My ears start ringing and I feel my blood rush to my head.

His leg. Just below the knee. It's gone.

His leg is gone.

It's too much. I feel my body sway and Dillon curses next to me as I start to fall. I don't remember anything else.

CHAPTER 22

I wake up in my bed. I'm not sure how I got there, but I do remember a little. A man's face keeps popping into my head. A paramedic. I remember his blue shirt and kind eyes.

"Oakley?"

I tense and look to the right. Mom is sitting on my bed.

She moves closer to me and reaches out, pushing my hair out of my face. "How are you feeling?"

Carson. The shark. The blood. His missing leg. My stomach turns and I feel like I'm going to throw up. "Is Carson okay?" It's barely a whisper.

Mom hesitates.

I push her hand away from my hair and sit up. "Is Carson okay?"

She sighs. "We don't know. He lost a lot of blood." She hesitates again and I know he's not doing well from the way she looks at me. "He's in a coma."

No. This can't be happening. He can't die. He can't. He's all I have now. I can't lose him too. I can't! Why did I try and push him away?

This is my fault. If I wouldn't have been so stupid and selfish, none of this would have happened.

I cover my mouth to stifle a sob. I don't know what else to do. My body shakes and I'm freezing. I swear I'm going to pass out again.

It should have been me.

But it's never me. Things always happen to the people I love most.

Why couldn't it have been me?

"It's going to be okay," Mom says. She wraps her arms around me as I cry and I lean into her and sob. I cry for Carson. I cry for Lucas. I cry for Mom and Dad. I cry for me. I cry until I run out of tears.

After what seems like forever, I finally pull away and lie down. My head hurts and my eyes sting.

"Do you need anything, honey?"

I shake my head.

She looks worried but stands. "Get some rest. I'll let you know if I hear anything else."

I don't answer, just curl in a ball and stare at nothing.

I'm not sure how long it's been. I don't remember falling asleep, but when I wake, it's light outside. Like, really light. Morning. My eyes are swollen. I can feel it. Avoiding looking in the mirror, I slide out of bed and tiptoe out to the porch. I stare at Carson's house. No cars are in the driveway. His family must be at the hospital—any family would be.

Part of me wants to go there too. I need to know how he's doing but I can't bring myself to go. After Lucas came home, I told myself I'd never go into another hospital again. It's too much.

I don't know what to do, so I sit down in a wicker chair and wait for something to happen.

Nothing does. The hours pass by in silence as I stare across the street at the ocean. It looks so calm. Like nothing bad could ever happen there. It's deceiving, the ocean. One second you can be swimming along and the next . . .

I swallow and shake my head. Don't think about it. Maybe if I don't think about it, it will all go away. Maybe it's all a dream.

Jo pokes her head out the door and tells me lunch is ready. I don't say anything and she disappears back inside. She comes out a few minutes later and sets a plate on the table beside me.

"You need to eat something."

She stands there, waiting for me to say something, but I don't. I'm not hungry. I don't even look to see what she's made. She sighs and goes back inside, leaving me alone.

Someone opens the door behind me, steps on to the porch, and sits down next to me. Mom. I don't know what she wants but I'm not in the mood to talk to anyone.

"How are you doing?" she asks.

I don't answer.

"Honey, Jo said Carson's sister's called several times. You should probably call her back."

Poor Keilani. She's probably having a horrible time. I know what it feels like to watch a brother die. My eyes burn but I swallow and breathe slowly to calm myself down. "I can't."

"She thinks if you go to the hospital, maybe if he hears your voice . . ."

I'm shaking my head before she finishes. I can't go. I can't see him hooked up to all those monitors. I've seen it before. It's too much.

"Oakley—"

"No," I say softly.

"Why?"

"What you're asking . . . there's no way," I say, my voice shaky. "I can't go there." I stand and walk toward the door. "I've already lost Lucas. I can't watch Carson die too. I can't go back to that place again."

"I'll be right by you, honey. I promise."

Still, I shake my head.

She sighs. "This is my fault."

I glance at her. "What?"

"This. You. I'm sorry, Oakley. I'm so sorry for everything. For not being there for you. For thinking I was the only one allowed to grieve. You're the way you are because of me."

"No. It's my own fault. I pushed everyone away."

"So did I . . ." she says.

We're both quiet until she looks up at me. "Do you love him?"

Do I? Do I love him? "I don't know," I whisper. "Maybe."

"Then why—"

"I just can't." I can feel the walls I've been so careful to build around myself start to crumble. The sea of emotions trying to escape makes it hard to breathe. My chest rises and falls and I take a step back. "I need to get out of here." I push the door open and slam it behind me.

I hear her following but don't stop. "What do you mean? Where are you going?"

I ignore her. Panic fills my body and I know I'm about to freak out. I can't stay here. I have to get away. Go to the only other place I know that can help me forget. I run to my room and grab Lucas's notebook and my purse.

"Oakley, stop. Please. What are you doing?"

"I'm going home." I grab Jo's keys off the table and run out the front door. I hear Mom yelling behind me but I jump in the car and lock the doors before she can stop me. The last thing I see as I peel out of the driveway is her standing on the porch, staring after me.

The airport is packed. Maybe it's always this way though. I don't fly very often.

I stare at the plane ticket in my hand, trying to ignore my fluttery stomach. It's fine. Everything's fine. If I go home, it will be like none of this ever happened. I never lived with Aunt Jo. I never learned to surf. I never fell for Carson.

It'll be easier to forget.

My cell rings again and I ignore it. I know it's Mom or Jo. I know they're probably freaking out but I don't have a choice. And I can ride on a plane by myself. I'm just going home. I don't even have any baggage to check.

An airline staff member calls business class and passengers traveling with young children into the plane. I stare at the seat number on my boarding pass.

Seat 28E, boarding group C. I hope they call my section soon.

I know I should have thought this through a little more. I'm never this spontaneous. If you could call it that. I wonder what Mom is thinking but then shake my head. She'll be fine.

I pull out my cell and I'm just about to call Dad to tell him I'm coming home when I see them.

They're young. Probably my age. The girl has long dark hair and the guy has light brown. I have no idea who they are but the way they move together makes me stare.

They're holding hands as they walk down the terminal, smiling. They stop a few feet away from me and the guy pulls out his boarding pass, looks it over, and hands it to the girl. He says something to her, making her laugh, and she playfully pushes him away. He reaches out and wraps an arm around her shoulders, pulling her close. She laughs again as he kisses her head. After a moment, oblivious to anyone else in the building, they give each other the sweetest kiss I've ever seen. He touches her cheek and brushes the hair from her face. It's as though the world has stopped for them and they're the only two people who matter. They break from their moment and he kisses her hand as they settle into a slow walk again.

It's a beautiful moment. I want to have a moment like that, where nothing else matters but the person I'm sharing it with. Do I love Carson? Is it possible to fall in love so fast?

The woman at the desk calls the next group of passengers to the line, making me panic a bit. I've already bought my ticket, so I can't turn back, but I'm starting to have second thoughts about my decision. Ignoring the thoughts running through my head, I stand and make my way over to hand her my ticket. Her lipstick is really red and her light hair is pulled into a tight bun. She's young, maybe twenty. I watch her scan my ticket into her computer and she hands it back to me with a smile on her face. "Have a nice flight," she says.

"Thanks," I mumble.

I start down the gangway, wringing my hands. Am I doing the right thing? Am I a coward? I don't stop. I can't. My feet keep moving and I make it all the way to my seat before sitting down between a large man who smells like bacon and a mean-looking old lady.

Carson's face appears in my mind. His smile. The dimple in his cheek. It's no wonder I fell for him. I rub my arms as a chill fills my body and I cringe as another image of him pops into my head. The shark. The blood. My screams. I shiver. I wonder how many tubes and IVs he's hooked up to in the hospital.

I think of Lucas. All of our memories. The good, the bad. And that's when I remember the notebook stuffed in my purse. I pull it out. If there's one thing I need right now, it's Lucas.

DEAR OAKLEY,

LIFE ISN'T FAIR. YOU KNOW THIS. I KNOW THIS. YET WE ALWAYS WONDER WHY BAD THINGS HAPPEN TO GOOD PEOPLE.

LIFE IS HARD. BUT THERE ARE SO MANY THINGS WE CAN LEARN WHEN WE'RE GOING THROUGH HARD THINGS. TAKE ME, FOR EXAMPLE. I'VE LEARNED HOW MUCH A PERSON CAN CARE FOR SOMEONE ELSE. I'VE LEARNED TO TREASURE EACH MOMENT I HAVE WITH THOSE I LOVE. I'VE LEARNED TO NOT TAKE THINGS FOR GRANTED. A HANDSHAKE FROM A FRIEND. A CONVERSATION. EVEN SOMETHING AS SIMPLE AS TAKING A BREATH.

I'VE LEARNED THAT EVEN THOUGH IT'S HARD, LIFE MATTERS. IT COULD HAVE BEEN EASIER TO JUST RUN AWAY FROM MY LIFE, BUT YOU'VE KEPT ME HOLDING ON. YOU'RE NOT READY TO LET GO OF ME YET, AND TO BE HONEST, YOU'RE JUST AS MUCH OF A FIGHTER IN MY BATTLE AS I AM.

WHEN I'M GONE, DON'T RUN AWAY FROM LIFE. EVEN IF IT'S HARD. IT'S FULL OF LESSONS. AND HAPPINESS. AND GOOD THINGS. DON'T THROW IT AWAY. THINGS GET HARD, AND THINGS AREN'T FAIR, BUT IF YOU'RE WILLING TO FACE YOUR PROBLEMS HEAD ON, THINGS WILL GET BETTER. THEY'LL WORK OUT. AND I KNOW YOU'LL WORK THROUGH WHATEVER OBSTACLES COME YOUR WAY. AT LEAST PROMISE ME YOU'LL TRY. YOU'VE SHOWN ME EXACTLY WHAT YOU CAN DO THIS PAST MONTH. BELIEVE IN YOURSELF. I BELIEVE IN YOU.

LOVE, LUCAS

I reread the letter three more times.

He forgot to mention that life sucks. But I guess that's the same as not being fair.

Lucas is right. As he usually is. If he says I can get through anything, I can get through anything. I can't abandon Carson. No matter how hard it might be to see him in pain, I can't do that to him. Not after all we've been through. Surfing, guitars, walks on the beach. The perfect spring full of memories that I'll never be able to forget.

If he dies before I can say goodbye . . .

I gulp and it hits me. Lucas would be so disappointed in me right now. He never would have abandoned me and neither would Carson.

I stand and squeeze past the big guy and make it into the aisle. I have to get out of here. I can be strong. I can help Carson fight. I can be the person I was when Lucas was fighting for *his* life. To help him up when he's down.

To keep him hanging on when it's so much easier to let go. I won't lose him. I won't let him go. Not yet.

Life isn't fair but it is worth fighting for.

I walk toward the door, muttering apologies to everyone as I make my way back through the gangway and into the airport. I've made up my mind. There's only one place for me to be right now.

With Carson.

CHAPTER 23

I step through the hospital doors. I've never been in this particular hospital but they all smell the same. Disinfectant. Antiseptic. Disease.

The smell triggers memories of Lucas lying in his hospital bed and makes me so dizzy that I almost fall over. I steady myself against the wall and take a deep breath, trying to ignore the memories of medicines, sickness, and death.

A nurse sits at a big desk and I walk over to her. I swallow the lump in my throat. I can do this. I can be brave.

"May I help you?" Her voice is nice. Pretty and light. She reminds me of my grandma with wispy white hair and glasses on the bridge of her nose.

"I'm here to see a patient. Carson Nye?"

She looks in her computer and gives me a sympathetic look. "Shark attack, right?"

I nod and swallow again.

"He's in the ICU."

"Oh. Okay." I'm not sure how to get in there and know they probably won't let me in. I step away but then hear a familiar voice.

"Oakley?"

Keilani walks over to me and wraps me in a huge hug. "Oh, Oakley, I'm so glad you're here," she says. She wipes a tear away as she lets me go. She looks exhausted.

All I can do is nod to keep myself from crying again.

The lady at the desk doesn't say anything as Keilani leads me down the hall. We step in the elevator and she pushes the second floor button.

"I didn't think you were going to come," she says. "Carson told me about your brother. I'm sure this is hard for you."

"I'm fine." For now.

The doors slide open and we walk into a waiting room. Carson's parents are there, of course, but they haven't noticed us yet.

It takes me a minute to catch my breath because the scene looks so familiar. It reminds me of when my parents and I would wait for one of Lucas's surgeries to be over. We'd usually stay in the waiting room for hours, waiting for the doctors to come tell us how it went. It happened more times than I like to remember.

I take in the scene again and try to keep my emotions in check. From the fake flowers in the large vase next to the couch and the warm lighting that gives me a headache if I'm in there too long, to the empty Styrofoam cups sitting on the coffee table. I stare at the one with teeth marks all around the edge. That would have been mine.

I glance at Carson's mother, who is reading a magazine in one of the chairs. She looks exhausted. Her dark hair is in a messy bun and it looks like she doesn't have makeup on. His father snores softly on the couch across the room, his feet up on the table in front of him and his arms behind his head.

"Look who I found," Keilani says, interrupting the silence.

Carson's mom looks up and her eyes widen when she sees me. "Oakley, thank you so much for coming." She gets up and gives me a hug. His dad stirs on the couch, opening his eyes for a second, but says nothing and doesn't bother getting up to greet me.

Carson's mom pulls away but takes my hand. I'm not sure if I want to know the answer but I want to be brave, so I ask. "How's he doing?"

She sighs. "He's still in a coma. They've given him a transfusion since he lost so much blood. Four pints. His heart stopped twice on the way to the hospital." Her lip quivers and she clears her throat and steadies herself. "But they were able to bring him back. He's in critical condition, but breathing on his own. They're just waiting for him to wake up now to see if he . . . if he has any brain damage."

I nod. I don't want to think about what will happen if he doesn't wake up.

"Would you like to see him?" she asks.

"Yes," I say before I can think about it or talk myself out of it.

"Two people are allowed back there at a time but I wonder if you'd rather go by yourself."

"I'd like that. If it's all right." I don't want to cry in front of anyone. And I will cry.

"Let me see when it's okay to go back. Why don't you sit with Keilani for a bit?"

"Okay." I follow Keilani over to the empty couch. She sits down and pulls her knees to her chest. She looks so lost. So scared. I'm not sure how to make her feel better. "How are you holding up?"

She shakes her head. "Honestly, I've never been so scared in my entire life."

I nod. "He'll be okay."

"Just the . . . blood. His leg. I can't get it out of my head."

"I can't either."

"I'm so glad you were there. You saved his life, Oakley. He would have died if you wouldn't have been with him."

He still might.

She glances over and gives me a small smile. "Carson's a pain in the butt most of the time but he's my big brother. I don't know what I'd do without him. I just . . . "

"I know." I swallow, hard. I totally understand.

The nurse walks over then, along with Carson's mom. "You ready to go back?" the nurse asks.

Yes. I can do this.

"I think so."

I stand.

"We'll be right out here," Carson's mom assures me. I smile and nod at her.

"Hey," Keilani says. "When you're done in there, would you want to grab some lunch or something? I need to get out of here for a bit and I'd love for you to come with me. I just. . . I don't want to be alone."

"Of course."

She smiles and sits back on the couch for a moment before her worried expression returns.

I follow the nurse back to his room. The walls are white. It smells like everything has been soaked in Lysol and sanitizer. We reach a room and she pulls a curtain back to let me in. I freeze in the doorway. My body shakes. I'm not sure if I can move.

The nurse is watching me. "It's all right."

"I know," I say. Even though it's not. At all.

"You can stay in here as long as you'd like. He may be in a coma, but he can hear you. I've been at this hospital twenty years and almost every person that has come out of a coma said they could hear people around them. Talk to him. Let him know you're here." She smiles. "I'll be right outside. Let me know if you need anything," she says. And then it's just the two of us.

I take a deep breath and move closer. Carson is surrounded by monitors and bags of fluid. I see the heart rate monitor go up and down and up and down. At least his heart is still beating. That's all I want to see for now.

I walk over to him and sit next to his bed. An oxygen tube is in his nose and I watch his chest rise and fall a few times just to be sure he's breathing.

I've been in this situation before. With Lucas. Though Lucas was bone thin and white as a sheet. He was so weak toward the end he could barely lift his hand. I shake my head to get the memories out and focus on Carson instead.

"Carson," I say. "It's Oakley." I take his hand in mine, careful of the IV. I'm not sure what else to say. I bring his hand to my lips and then rest it on the bed again. I don't let go.

I take a deep breath and start talking. "I've been thinking about the first time we met. You know, when I almost fell in the tide pool? I'll never admit this to your face . . . well, I guess I am now, but I thought you were so hot. It was why I didn't talk a lot. I didn't know what to say." I smile at the memory. "I've never been good around guys. As you can probably tell. But you didn't seem to notice. You were so nice. Too nice, I thought. Then when you took me to see the pier and introduced me to the best hot dog I've ever tasted, I knew I wanted to get to know you more. I'm glad I have that memory as our first date. You can take me there again when you're better. I'm buying this time though.

"Remember how I totally ate it when you taught me how to surf for the first time? I swear there's still salt stuck in my nose. I was seriously horrible. And I know you won't say it, but we both know I still am." I chuckle quietly and look to see if there is any response.

Nothing.

"But the thing I remember most is the night you kissed me. When we sat in my room playing the guitar. It was the perfect moment. I was terrified that I'd mess it up. That I wouldn't kiss you right, but it was . . . like magic. A perfect kiss. I'll never forget that night."

I lean in closer and brush his hair out of his closed eyes. "Please come back to me. I don't want to lose you." A tear rolls down my cheek and I climb on the bed next to him, careful not to touch his body or get near his injured leg. I lay my head next to his and touch his face, letting my emotions take over, letting it all out. I'm still holding his hand. "I think I love you," I whisper, knowing he probably can't hear.

I don't know how long I lie beside him. Minutes. Hours. I've memorized every sound, every beep from the monitors around us. The deep breaths he takes and the beat of his heart.

I've been in here for a while. I should leave so his family can come back in. I touch my lips to his cheek and slide off the bed. "I'll be back tomorrow," I say. "I promise." I feel a twitch in his hand. Just a small one. My heart speeds up and I look down to see his hand slowly wrap around mine.

A new round of tears are falling freely as I watch his chest rise and fall again. My eyes look back at our hands intertwined. He doesn't let go and I know it's not a reflex. He knows I'm with him. And then I remember his family. I need to tell them or a nurse that he responded. I stand to leave and he squeezes my hand again. He doesn't open his eyes or move or anything but he's still squeezing my hand tight.

"I'll be right back," I say. I rush through the curtain and into the hall. A nurse is standing at the desk and when she sees me, her eyes widen. "What's wrong?"

"He squeezed my hand," I say.

She walks quickly into the room and I follow her. She checks a few monitors and his IV fluids. She lifts his sheets on her side so I can't see his wounds but I look away anyway. When she's done, she motions for me to follow her out of the room.

"This is a great sign. Usually people don't make responses that fast once they slip into a coma. He's making great progress already. I'm going to call his doctor. You should probably tell his family he's responding. Even if it was only squeezing your hand."

"Thank you," I say.

She gives me a funny look. "You're his girlfriend, right?"

I'm not sure, but I nod anyway. It'll take me a while to get used to "girlfriend."

She smiles. "I'm glad you came. It's amazing what love can do for a person, isn't it?"

I smile. "It really is."

CHAPTER 24

The first thing I notice about the next letter is that it's in my mom's handwriting and not Lucas's. I frown and flip to the next page. There's nothing there. A lump forms in my throat as I realize this is the last letter in my notebook. And obviously he was in too much pain to write it. I'm not sure if I can read it. Not yet. I tuck it under my pillow again and roll out of bed.

Mom and Jo are in the kitchen. Mom walks over and gives me a small hug before returning to her seat. "Carson's mom called this morning."

"And?"

"He's awake."

My heart leaps in my chest. He's awake. He's really awake. I can't believe it. "Did they say anything else? Is he okay? Is he talking at all?"

Jo laughs as she sets down her coffee. "He's asking for you."

I clear my throat and focus on Jo's coffee mug to keep my crazy emotions in check. "Really?" I sniff and Mom reaches out a hand and touches my arm.

"Why don't you eat something and I'll drive you to the hospital?" she asks. She never said a word when I came home last night. Didn't yell at me, didn't ground me. All she did was hug me and tell me to get some sleep. She loves me. I know that now. And all this time I know it's really been *me* pushing *her* away.

I look at her and nod. It's all I can do to keep from crying. "I'm not very hungry. Can we go now?"

Mom sighs. "Honey, you can't not eat."

"Please?"

She glances at Jo, but nods. "Okay. Get dressed and we'll go as soon as you're ready."

I take five minutes to put on some clothes and throw my unruly hair into a messy bun. Jo hands me a granola bar on our way out the door. We arrive at the hospital ten minutes later.

Carson is still in intensive care. We walk down the narrow hallway and the nurse from the night before recognizes me. "You're here to see Carson?"

"Yes."

I look around for his family but don't see anyone.

She smiles. "His family went to get some sleep. I'm sure they'll be back soon. They've barely left the hospital since the accident. Sweet things. I'll take you on back, honey."

I glance at Mom. "Go ahead," she says. "I'll be right here."

The nurse motions for me to follow her and I wave goodbye to Mom. It's nice to have her with me. We've both been through a lot. Too much, if you ask me.

Maybe with that one thing in common, we'll make it. We have to.

We stop in front of his room and the nurse pokes her head inside. I'm twisting my hands in front of me. I'm not supposed to be nervous. It's not like I don't know him.

"Go on in. He's waiting for you."

I take a huge breath and step inside the curtain.

I thought he'd be lying down but he's sitting on his bed, propped up by several pillows. His brown eyes find mine as soon as I walk in, and even though he's really pale, his smile lights up the room. His chest rises and he breathes a sigh of what sounds like relief.

"You're okay," he says.

My heart feels like it will burst out of my chest as I rush to the side of his bed When I reach him, he slowly raises a hand and I take it, pulling it to my lips. "*You're* okay," I whisper.

He lets go of my hand and pats the bed next to him. "Come sit."

"But—"

"It's okay. I'm okay. Well . . ." He glances toward his legs. "Sort of, I guess."

I'm careful as I climb on the bed next to him, steering clear of his legs. I lean my head against his chest and wrap my arms carefully around him. He sniffs and I feel warm tears on my cheek. I'm not sure if they're mine or his.

"I was so scared," I whisper. "So, so scared."

He strokes my hair. "Me too."

We sit there for a long time, neither of us saying a word. The nurse walks in then, changes the bag of fluid hooked to his IV, and walks back out without a word. I'm glad she's letting us have this moment.

"I'm so sorry, Carson."

"It's not your fault."

I pull away and sit back, still hanging on to his hand. "Does it hurt?" I don't know why I ask when I'm sure it does.

He shrugs. "It's no big deal." I see a hint of a smile. I don't know how he can joke about it but I smile anyway.

"You've been attacked by a shark before?"

"Nope. I'll admit this is a first." He's trying to make light of things but I can see the pain in his eyes.

I squeeze his hand. "How bad is it?"

He closes his eyes for a second. "I can't feel it right now. Too much medication. I'm surprised I'm even awake and talking to you." He takes a deep breath. "I know my leg is gone. I knew before I woke up. I heard the doctors talking while I was asleep."

My lip quivers and I fight to keep my emotion back. I don't know what to say, so I just sit there, staring at our hands.

"Oakley," he whispers. I look up at his serious expression. "I'm gonna be okay," he says. "Okay?"

"But . . . your leg." My voice cracks and I bury my face in his shoulder. Why do things like this have to happen to people I love? After watching Lucas suffer for so long, I can't bear to see Carson do it too. Because even though Carson's situation is different—he at least knows he's going to live—to lose his leg? I don't want to see him in so much pain.

"Oakley," Carson says.

I look up and meet his eyes again.

"I'm alive. You're alive. That's all that matters. I'll figure out what to do about my leg another time, but for now, I'm thankful we're still here. Together."

He's right. I try to push the thought of him not being able to walk or surf again out of my head. It's hard, but I manage.

Carson's quiet for a moment before squeezing my hand. "Let's talk about something . . . happy."

I nod and ask him the first thing that pops into my mind. "Where's your family?"

He smiles. "I told them to go home for a while."

"Your dad . . ." I start.

"I know."

I look up, surprised. "You do?"

"Lani told me you heard. I'm sorry."

"Oh . . ."

"Don't worry about him, okay? I'll take care of it. Once he gets over the fact that I'm doing something else with my life, he'll be fine. He just wants what he thinks is best for me. He really is a nice guy, just a little overbearing at times. Unfortunately, you haven't seen the nice part yet, but it's there."

I find it strangely reassuring that he's talking about what he's going to do with his life. He's going to be fine. I know it. Even though his leg is gone, he's still thinking about his future. And why wouldn't he be? I should be doing the same thing.

He yawns and leans back on his pillow.

"I'm going to let you get some rest." I swing my legs over the side of the bed but he holds tight to my hand when I try to pull away.

"Don't go. Not yet." His expression is pained. "Please."

I settle back on the bed next to him. "Okay, I won't leave unless you make me."

"Have fun spending every night with me then." I climb in next to him and he puts his arm—the one that isn't hooked to an IV—around me. I lean against his chest and smile as I hear the wonderful thump of his heart.

I roll my eyes. "Like the nurses or your parents would let that happen."

He shrugs. "I'm sure they'd be fine. It's not like I can take advantage of you anyway. I'm too loopy to do anything but lie here."

I let out a laugh, complete with a snort. I cover my mouth and close my eyes, humiliated.

Carson laughs too, although every movement looks like it causes him pain. When he stops laughing, he looks over at me. "That was cute. You should do it more often."

I raise an eyebrow. "Snort?"

"Very attractive."

"Lucas hated it when I did that. He said I sounded like a guy."

"I don't snort and I'm a guy."

"Great. What does that make me then?"

He chuckles and pulls my hand up to his lips to kiss the back of it. "It means you're beautiful. Snorting or not."

"That makes me feel a little better. I guess."

The nurse walks in again and glances at the two of us. "I need to check Carson's wound now. You probably don't want to be here when I do that, so you're welcome to hang out in the waiting room for a bit."

"She can stay," he says.

I squeeze his hand, reassuring him that I'm not going anywhere. "Yeah. I think I will."

CHAPTER 25

The ride home is quiet, save for Mom's music on the radio. I'm tired. I stayed at the hospital all day and only left because the nurses kicked me out so Carson could sleep.

I glance over at Mom. She looks tired too. "Thanks for taking me today."

"You're welcome."

I sit for a moment and finally get the courage to speak. "You knew about Lucas's notebook. You wrote in it."

She doesn't say anything, just nods and stares at the road.

"Why didn't you tell me he was keeping something like that?"

"He made me swear not to tell you."

I could just hear him making her swear some kind of oath or something. I smile. "Sounds like him."

"Have you finished it yet?"

"No. I can't bring myself to read the last entry."

"Read it. He loved you, Oakley. Every time you weren't at the hospital, he'd keep asking when you were going to come. I'm pretty sure you're the one he was staying here for. You were his best friend. I hope you know how much you meant to him."

"He meant more to me," I say. And he did. Lucas taught me so many things about myself. Before he got sick, when he was sick, and even now. He wasn't afraid to do things. He wasn't afraid to just be himself. He saw the good in everything. And from reading his notebook every day, his happiness and the optimistic way he looked at the world is starting to rub off on me. "I miss him."

"Me too." She smiles and then opens her mouth to say something else, but closes it. I know what she's going to say and I beat her to it.

"I'm sorry," I say.

"Oakley—"

"No. I'm sorry for everything. I've been a horrible daughter. I've made all of this harder on you, Mom. Lucas, Dad. I . . . I'm so sorry. I just miss Lucas so much and I took everything out on you. I didn't understand how much you were hurting too."

"It's not your fault, Oakley."

"A lot of it is. You've done nothing but love me. And I pushed you away. Dad, too. And everyone at home. I'm such an idiot."

"You're not an idiot. And if anyone should be apologizing, it's me."

"You don't have to apologize for anything."

"I do. I'm sorry I wasn't there when Lucas was going through everything. I wasn't ready to lose him. I didn't know how to talk to you about it and I know I abandoned you." Tears fill her eyes and she blinks, letting them spill down her cheeks. "I'm so sorry. And I didn't realize how much the divorce would affect you either. I feel awful."

"I understand, Mom. Really."

"I love you, honey. I want you to know that. I really truly do. I don't know what I'd do without you, and . . . I'm going to make all those lost months up to you. I'm going to fix this."

I reach over and grab her hand. "I love you too. And we'll fix it together."

CHAPTER 26

I stare at the notebook again. I've pulled it out so many times, but for some reason, I can't seem to get a hold of myself long enough to read the last letter. The handwriting is not Lucas's. That means it's the last thing he wanted to say to me before he died. And that means the letters will be over and I'll have nothing else to look forward to reading from him. All the advice and memories will stop and I'm afraid I'll fall back into my depression. I don't want them to end. I don't want it to be over.

But I want to know what he says.

The notebook sits in my hands for almost fifteen minutes. I'm still staring at it, wondering what could be in his last message for me. I take a shaky breath and open it.

Dear Oakley,

As you already know, this isn't my handwriting. Mom's writing it for me, since I can't do anything on my own anymore. My time's almost up. I can feel it. My body is shutting down, and honestly, I welcome it. I'm not afraid to die. It's a whole new adventure I'm ready to face.

In all seriousness, I want to tell you something. Don't ever lose hope. Even when a situation is the worst you could ever think of, hope will always pull you through. It's been a constant companion through the last few months, and even though I know I'm not going to make it, I still have hope that I can leave some good in this world.

And about me leaving. People will grow old, move on, forget about me, but I know you won't. You've been by my side, hoping, praying for me this whole time. And I want to tell you how much it has meant to me.

I look forward to our visits every day. You always lift me up and pull me back. Your happiness is contagious. Please don't lose it. I know there are so many people whose lives you'll touch. So many people who will meet you for one second and want to know everything about you. You have that effect on people. Your smile, your laugh. Even your ugly snort. But all kidding aside, you're beautiful inside and out.

I know you're going to have a hard time when I'm gone. You'll miss me. And trust me when I say I'll miss you too. We've been through so much together, it's only natural. But don't let you missing me stop you from doing the things you were meant to do. You're going to be great in this world, Oakley. I can feel it. You're the reason I'm still here. Not even kidding. Without you, I would have given up ages ago. So, don't lose that spark. Don't lose hope. Be true to yourself and move on with your life. Don't carry the past along with you, but don't forget it either. And don't forget about me.

I love you little sis.

Love, Lucas

I'm crying so hard, I can't even read the words on the page anymore. I try to wipe my tears away as fast as they fall, but it isn't fast enough. I close the notebook and lie on my bed, burying my face in my pillow. I need to cry. I need to let it all out and then I can get myself under control and figure out what to do next.

Hours pass. My eyes are swollen and red. I have a headache. My pillow is soaking wet where I've been lying and my body is sore from sobbing. I sit up and pull my sticky hair away from my face and sniff.

Lucas is right. It's time to move on. I need to take control of my life. Be there for Carson as he goes through physical therapy. Be there for Mom and Dad, even if I don't agree with their decisions. I'm an adult now. I'll be eighteen in a few weeks and it's time to figure out what I want to do with my life.

I turn the page of the notebook and grab a pen.

CHAPTER 27

The hospital isn't busy at all. I go to the intensive care unit and look around for the nurse who's usually there. She sees me and waves me over. "We transferred him to another room. Don't worry, it's a good thing. It means the doctors think he's stable enough and doing well enough to function without all those machines." She walks behind the big desk and pulls out a clipboard. "He's in room 220, on the second floor. Go right in. I'm sure he's expecting you."

I release the breath I'm holding and she smiles. It occurs to me that I've never learned her name. "Thank you," I say. "Can I get your name? I'm sorry I haven't asked before."

"No worries. It's Michelle."

"Thank you so much, Michelle. For everything."

"Anytime. You take care of that boy, you hear? He's a keeper from what I've seen."

"Yes. He is."

Carson's sitting up and eating lunch when I arrive at the hospital. A grin spreads across his face as I walk into the room. "Hey," he says and pushes his tray away.

"Don't stop eating because of me."

"No, I'm just finishing up. And have you ever tasted hospital food?" He makes a face and sticks out his tongue.

I laugh. Lucas had hated it too.

"How are you feeling today?"

He moves and flinches, but acts like he's fine. "Good."

I frown. "For real."

"Better."

"You don't have to be brave in front of me."

He searches my face for a moment and his eyes water. He shakes his head and reaches for my hand. "You know, I've been pretty good at being optimistic about this whole thing. But when everyone leaves and goes home, the doubt creeps in. I can't get rid of it. It's like it's torturing me until I admit that I . . . that I'm scared."

He doesn't look at me, just stares at our hands intertwined on the bed. "I know I'm going to be okay, but I have a long recovery. They're sending me home soon and I start physical therapy in a few weeks to learn how to strengthen my left leg since I can't use my right anymore." He cringes. "Every time I move it, it's torture right now. My doctor says it will be bad for a while. And after it heals, I'll get something called phantom pains." He takes a deep breath and gives me a smile. "I just have to take it one day at a time. You know?"

"I know."

"I'll probably never surf again. Which sucks." His shoulders sag and he sighs. "I'll figure it out." He looks up at me and smiles. "How are you today? Anything exciting happening out in the world?"

I can't help but laugh, and then I go quiet. I came here to tell him something and I need to do it before I chicken out. "I read Lucas's last letter today."

"From that notebook?"

"Yes."

"Are you okay?"

"I think so. I know I will be, eventually. It's only been a month or so since he died, but I feel like I'm going to be okay. My emotions are still all over the place. So . . . raw. All I felt after he died was grief and I didn't know what else to feel. It grabbed onto my heart and squeezed until almost nothing was left. It almost took over my life. Until I met you."

"Me?"

"Not the first time I met you, but as I started to get to know you. You've helped me be myself again. And I'm sorry you had to see my depressed and grieving self. It wasn't pretty. I know that now. And I'm going to try to leave it behind. I don't know why you started to like me in the first place."

He chuckles. "First of all, I love how enthusiastic you are about the world around you. How you try new things. Jumping in the ocean to surf for the first time and never looking back, Rollerblading, even though you were certain you'd crash—biking, too. Trying to teach me the guitar, the way you take pictures of everything and hang them on your wall. Picking up a starfish, not just to pick it up, but to examine it because it's cool. You view things in your own way and I love that about you. And the way you care about those you love and will do anything to protect them. I not only saw that during the shark attack, but what you've told me about your relationship with your brother is priceless. Staying with him day after day in that hospital just so he wouldn't be lonely? You're loyal and selfless and will do anything for people you love. And, when I break down all your walls and get you to actually talk to me, you're real. Not some fake who's just trying to nab a boyfriend. You're genuine. You don't pretend to be someone you're not. I could keep going . . ."

I'm quiet for a second, gathering my thoughts. "Can I tell you something?"

"Of course."

I remember Lucas's letters. His advice in each one. Now is my chance to use it. I pull a stack of pictures out of my purse and give them to him. "Actually, before I do, I wanted you to have these."

He takes the photographs and flips through them, moisture filling his eyes. "This is me."

"Yes."

All of them are pictures of Carson surfing. I wanted to capture every detail, every movement, and he had no idea I was even there. It made the pictures even better because he was just being himself. Not trying to impress anyone.

"When did you take these?"

I shrug. "When I was avoiding you I'd take walks on the beach and see you out there. I'm not a stalker, I swear."

"These are . . ." His voice cracks. "Amazing."

"I wanted you to have something to remember how it felt to be in the waves. Maybe you'll get out there again someday, but for now . . ."

He grabs my hand. "Thank you. You have no idea how much these mean to me."

"You're welcome." I blush and look away. I mentally prepare myself for what comes next. I look back at him. "There's something else."

"Okay?"

I clear my throat. "I've never been one to say how I feel. You've probably noticed that more than once—I don't like to talk about things. Never have. But I have to tell you this." I meet his eyes and my heart is beating so fast, it's getting hard to breathe. "I think . . ." I stop and shake my head. "I mean, I know . . ." I stop again. How do I say this without sounding like a total moron?

"I think there may be a small chance . . . a tiny one . . . that I might be . . . actually . . ." I shake my head and smile. I'm ridiculous. "I think I'm in love with you."

He's staring at me and his lips part slightly.

"I had to tell you. I don't want to regret not telling you."

His face softens and he breaks into a grin. "I don't think, I know," he says. "Since you fell off that first wave and went right back in, even after you were slammed into the beach, I knew."

I laugh. "That wasn't one of my finest moments."

"It was to me." He takes a deep breath and closes his eyes for a second.

"You're hurting. Can they give you any more pain medication?"

"Pretty sure I've used up all the morphine in the hospital."

"They gave you morphine?"

"Yep."

"I didn't know they still used that stuff."

"They do."

"How on Earth are you talking to me right now?"

He shrugs. "I'm not really sure. You do sound a little echoey though."

"That's it? I'd be curled up in a ball and rocking back and forth." I shiver. Heavy-duty medicine is not my friend. "One time I took some really strong cough syrup and when I blew my nose, cartoon characters came out."

He raises an eyebrow. "Were they green?"

I punch him in the arm—softly, since I swear he could break any second. "No. Like Mickey Mouse and his friends. I thought I was losing my mind."

"Uh . . . I'm pretty sure you were."

Great. Now he thinks I'm a crazy.

He closes his eyes again.

"I really should let you rest. I'm sure you need some sleep."

"I'm fine."

"Right." I stand and lean over, my lips hovering right above his. "Promise me you'll get some sleep. I'll be back later, okay? I need to have a chat with my mom. If I'm not back in a few hours, send help." I smile at the look he's giving me. "We just don't talk, so who knows what will happen."

"Okay. That makes more sense."

I lean down and touch his lips lightly with mine. I pull away and push his hair out of his eyes.

"Is that it?" he asks with a chuckle.

"For now. Go to sleep."

"You're no fun." His words are sort of slurred and he closes his eyes.

"I know. I'll see you later."

He's already snoring.

I step out of his room and find Mom. She's in the waiting room, just as she said she'd be. She's really focused on some soap opera on TV when I walk up.

"Enjoying yourself?" I ask.

She almost jumps out of her seat before turning to look at me. "Oh, you scared me." Her hand moves toward her chest and she takes a deep breath. "You're finished already?"

"He's tired. I told him I'd come back later."

"Oh. Good. Sleep is good."

"So . . . What do you want to do?"

"Why don't we go grab some lunch in the cafeteria? Then you can come back and hang out with Carson again."

"You really don't have to stay here and wait for me."

"I want to."

I reach out a hand and help her up. I surprise both of us when I wrap my arms around her and pull her into a hug. She hugs me back and we stay like that for a few minutes at least. When I pull away, she's smiling. "Thank you," she says.

I slip my arm through hers and lead her down the hallway. As we walk, I can't help but glance at her a few times to make sure she's real. She's been so absent in my life for so long, I'm not sure how she'll make up the time, but at least she's trying. And so am I.

CHAPTER 28

It's been six weeks since the attack. Carson's been doing physical therapy and has recovered very well. He's back to his old self, minus his leg. He's a pro on his crutches and has even gone back into the water at the beach. Not too far, but still. He's braver than I am.

I know Carson will be okay. The doctors want to fit him with a prosthetic leg eventually, so that's good. Days are long and frustrating for him being on crutches all the time but he's determined to make the best of it. And I know he will. He's just like that. Positive and always looking on the bright side. I wish I could do that. And I'm happy to say I'm working on it.

As we sit in Jo's boat, I grab Carson's hand, my nerves getting the best of me. He smiles at me before looking out into the water. "I really can't believe you're doing this. I thought you'd want to stay a million miles away from the ocean now."

"Seriously," Lani says. "My brother is officially crazy." She frowns and I give her half a smile.

Carson shakes his head and looks over at his sister. "I don't blame the shark, Lani. It's just a shark. I'm pretty sure it didn't think 'oh look, let's eat the human.'"

She frowns. "Still."

Jo stops the boat and I grimace as she pulls a chunk of raw meat out of a barrel. She attaches it to a hook and throws it out into the ocean.

"There have been quite a few great white sightings around here, so it shouldn't be long."

We sit in silence. The only sounds are the water smacking the side of the boat and Lani's humming.

Carson shifts next to me and stretches out his good leg. His other leg is wrapped like it usually is, just below the knee. It's healing nicely but it's hard for me to look at it. Not because it's gross or anything, but because the attack comes back full force in my mind. But no one needs to know that.

We sit and chat about Lani's surfing competition coming up and how Carson's physical therapy has been going. After about an hour goes by, I finally see it. A large dorsal fin coming slowly toward the boat.

"There's one," Jo says. "A big one."

Carson leans forward and rests his arm on the side of the boat. The shark circles where the piece of meat is, coming within a few feet of us.

I squeeze his hand. "You okay?"

He nods and squeezes back. "I'm fine," he says. "Even though one almost tore me apart. At the time I didn't realize how big they actually are."

I shiver. The shark swims by and it's easily ten to twelve feet long.

I glance at Carson, who's looking at me.

"Are *you* okay?" The corner of his mouth twitches.

"Yes. I'm fine. Why?"

"You're kind of squeezing my hand off."

"Oh!" I release my hold on his hand and he laughs.

"I keep hearing the *Jaws* music running through my head," Lani says. "It's starting to freak me out."

I glance at her. "Me too." For real.

It really is a sight to see though. Even if it's a scary one. I wonder if this shark is the one who bit Carson. There's no way to ever know.

The shark swims under the water and we lose sight of it until it appears under the piece of meat. It latches on with its huge jaws and shakes it in attempt to tear it off the hook. It lets go, swims around again, and goes right back to the meat, biting and tearing pieces off. Within minutes, there's nothing left.

I'm glad we're on a big boat. That thing could rip a small boat to pieces. I watch it swim around a little more and then it disappears under the water.

"That was awesome," Carson says.

"Are you kidding me?" I stare at him in disbelief. How can he be so calm when the animal that bit his leg off is swimming so close?

"What? It was." He pulls me to him and I lean against his chest. "It's okay, Oakley. I'm not gonna blame the shark. It didn't know what it was doing. I was just in the wrong place at the wrong time."

I nod and wonder why I'm feeling so many emotions. Sadness, anger, bitterness that this had to happen. I'm not even the one who lost my leg and I'm doing worse than he is.

He kisses my head as Jo reels in the fishing line and I work on pulling myself together.

"Doin' okay?" Jo asks.

"Fine," Carson says. "Thanks for bringing us out here. I needed this."

Jo smiles. "Anytime."

Jo drops us off at home a few hours later and Carson and I head to the beach. Carson's getting used to the crutches but it's still hard for him to maneuver them when they sink into the sand.

We head toward the pier and I gaze at the surfers in the water.

"You ever gonna go out again?" Carson asks.

I glance at him staring out into the waves. I smile and squeeze his hand. "Not any time soon."

To be honest, I don't know if I'll ever get in the ocean to surf again. The memories of the shark attack are too fresh in my mind to even think about it. But maybe in a few years. Or ten. Maybe someday I'll do it again. I'm definitely not counting it out forever.

Carson kisses my hand. "We'll have to find a new hobby to try."

"Yeah? Like what?"

He shrugs. "I don't know. Like chess or checkers."

I grin at him. "Seriously? Chess?"

He laughs. "Hey, it's something, right?"

It *is* something. I remember Lucas's words. *Learn something new.* I'll keep those words in mind in the coming years. I can do anything I put my mind to. And I'm sure I'll think of something great.

Carson's already on his way. He applied for an internship with Jo and signed up for his first semester of college in the fall. And his dad is supporting him. After the accident, his dad changed his mind about a few things. School, the shop, even me.

I wrap my arms around his waist and let out a peaceful sigh. I have everything I need right now. I'm in love with a boy who loves me back. I'm slowly picking up the pieces and putting my old self back together. Mom and I are on really good terms and Dad and I speak regularly. I've even drafted a few letters to my friends back home, though I haven't sent any yet. It will take time, I know, but in this moment, I'm content with where my life is heading.

I'll figure everything else out later.

CHAPTER 29

Dear Lucas,

It's kind of strange, writing you when you aren't here, but I had to do it. You have no idea how much your letters mean to me. I read one every day, even though I already know what they say. It brings me more comfort than you could ever imagine.

You were right. About everything. Especially the part where you said I'd miss you.

I miss you. It's true. It seems like yesterday we were skipping second period and going to Wendy's for Frosties. I always loved going with you and your friends. You always made me feel like I was your friend and not just your sister. Thanks for that.

I took your advice and told someone I loved him. And you know what? He loves me back. It's weird, and new and scary, but I'm welcoming it the best I can. We're good for each other. And he reminds me of you a little.

I'm sure you know about Mom and Dad getting divorced. It's been hard, but I'm slowly accepting it. Mom and I are doing well. We're working things out. Talking. Making up for lost time. Dad's good, too, though I don't see him as much as I'd like.

I'm figuring out what to do with college. I think I'm going to be a vet. I haven't decided for sure yet, but Aunt Jo said she could help me with some college applications and internships and stuff. It sounds promising. I've always loved animals. Oh, and I'm moving to Huntington Beach permanently. Just me and Mom. It will be a new adventure for us both. And no, I didn't decide to move there because of a guy.

There are so many things I want to say to your face. Like how I wish you could come see Jo's facility. You would love it. Or sit on the beach and watch the sunset with me. We would roast marshmallows and eat s'mores. But somehow, I can feel you with me. I know you're around, watching and rooting for me. I'm starting to move forward with my life, but like you said, I won't forget the past. It's too much a part of me to just let it go.

I hope you're enjoying your new adventure. I'm sure you are. I love and miss you every day. Thanks for always believing in me. I love you.

Love, Oakley

I set the letter next to Lucas's headstone and back away. Mom is on my right side with Dad on my left. For one small moment, we're all together. As a family.

Things won't ever be the same, I know that now, but at least I have this moment.

My life isn't perfect. It never will be. But I know I'm going to be okay. Trials make us stronger. Little by little. We just have to keep going and not give up hope. Just like Lucas said. As long as I have hope, everything will work out.

Dad gives me a squeeze and moves away, leaving Mom and me alone. She puts her arm around me. "We're going to be okay."

I nod, tears brimming my eyes. "I know." And I do.

She turns us both around and we walk back toward the car. Dad's waiting for us, with Carson by his side. They both smile at me and when I reach them, Carson takes my hand in his.

"Dad, will you join us for some ice cream before we head back to California?" I ask.

He looks at Mom and she gives him a small nod.

"I'd love to."

As we drive away, I squeeze Carson's hand as I look out the window. My eyes find Lucas's grave and the white and yellow flowers I left there. Maybe it was stupid to leave a letter with it when I know he'll never read it. I smile. Or maybe, just maybe, he already has.